a boy named
Walter

What others are saying about
A Boy Named Walter

"I can't tell you how much I enjoyed the book. It was beautifully written and conveys an amazing story that is 'spot on' for today's youth. I almost hate to admit it, being perhaps too much the jaded administrator, but I literally cried through parts of the book. How lucky we the readers are (and will be) to share this amazing adventure."

—Mark Geyer, Superintendent of Schools, California

"Wow! This is an amazing story! There are so many life lessons in this book. Students will see that in some way, shape, or form there is a 'Walter' in all of them."

—Linda Wilkinson, school principal
Sacramento County, California

"I was reminded of how much of an impact we, as educators, make in the lives of students every day. . . . I see students identifying with many of the adventures and feelings of Walter throughout the story. . . . I will highly recommend it to my teachers and students."

—Amy Banks, elementary school principal
Roseville, California

"I absolutely loved it! The stories were just phenomenal! It's a book anybody could read from older elementary students to adults."

—Cynthia Davis, teacher

"As a principal, I would want every one of my middle school students to read about Walter's journey! Walter inspires me to reach out to every student. This book changed my perspective!"

—Michelle Harmeier, principal
Coyote Ridge Elementary School
Dry Creek Joint Elementary School District

a boy named Walter

Les and Genny Nuckolls

Hegemony Press
An imprint of Cedar Fort, Inc.
Springville, Utah

The views expressed within this work are the sole responsibility of the author and do not necessarily reflect the position of Cedar Fort, Inc., or any other entity.

ISBN 13: 978-1-59955-932-2

Published by Hegemony Press, an imprint of Cedar Fort, Inc.
2373 W. 700 S., Springville, UT 84663
Distributed by Cedar Fort, Inc., www.cedarfort.com

LIBRARY OF CONGRESS CATALOGING-IN-PUBLICATION DATA
Nuckolls, Les, 1931- author.
A boy named Walter / Les & Genny Nuckolls.
p. cm.
Summary: A twelve-year-old boy runs away from his abusive foster home and hitchhikes to Sea View, California. He gets a job, signs up for school, and with the help of a compassionate widow, an understanding coworker, and some perceptive teachers, he lives on his own from then on.
ISBN 978-1-59955-932-2
1. Runaway children--Fiction. 2. Boys--Fiction. 3. Education--Fiction.
4. California--Fiction. I. Nuckolls, Genny, 1946- author. II. Title.

PS3614.U83B69 2011
813'.6--dc22

2011014905

Cover design by Danie Romrell
Cover design © 2011 by Lyle Mortimer
Edited and typeset by Stacy Owen

Printed in the United States of America

10 9 8 7 6 5 4 3 2 1

Printed on acid-free paper

This book is dedicated to Kris Comer, a teacher who embodies the kind of spirit that inspires students like Walter to find their way.

Books by Les and Genny Nuckolls

Growing Up in Africa
A Boy Named Walter

CONTENTS

One

RUN FOR YOUR LIFE

It was still dark outside. The sun had not yet lighted the flat farmland surrounding the little house. I stuffed my few clothes into my ragged backpack and tiptoed toward the back door. I was so frightened that my hands shook and my legs felt weak. *What if they should wake up?* I thought.

Down the hallway I could hear the farmer snoring, reassuring me that the uncaring old man and his cruel wife were still asleep.

Outside the morning air was cool, not hinting at the dry hot air that would soon smother this valley. By noon the temperature would be well above 100 degrees. At least in nearby Bakersfield there were some shade trees. Out here in the farm belt the largest tree was the olive, and it provided little or no protection from the relentless sun.

I had nearly completed the sixth grade in town when they moved me to this new foster home, miles from anywhere and with no neighbors in sight. As usual, I was given no reason why I had to leave the last home. Often it was because one of the foster parents had fallen ill or there was a divorce about to happen. My new guardians were poor farmers and they needed the small monthly check the county paid them to keep me, even though the word "keep" was a joke.

I'd had enough. Six foster homes in eight years, and now the seventh with this old lady who liked to slap kids around. Every night she boiled a vegetable like broccoli or cabbage and made it into a smelly mush. The odor of the rotting vegetable from the field was vile. "Hold your nose and take a bite," she instructed with a sneer. "You'll get used to it." Fighting the urge to gag, I would try to take a spoonful, but the foul smell would force me to run for the toilet and throw up. She would follow me into the bathroom and start slapping me around the head while screaming, "Go to bed, you ungrateful little bastard!"

With every step I took away from the house, a feeling of safety washed over me. I would be twelve years old soon and was leaving the broken-down farm and my life as a "ward of the court" of the county. No more abuse; I'd had enough. I was going out on my own, wherever that was.

As I walked across the field toward Highway 99, I looked up at the horizon above the distant mountains that I hoped I would soon cross. In past months the mountains were painted a brilliant spring yellow and blue when their ridges and valleys were covered with lush fields of poppies and lupines. Sometimes such an unexpected encounter with nature's beauty would bring a brief moment of peace and wonder into my life.

The sun was peeking down at the valley when I finally arrived at the highway. I sat my worn backpack down in the dirt beside the road and stuck out my right hand with the thumb up the way I'd seen hitchhikers do along this route. People in cars on their way to town looked at me with a puzzled expression when they passed. "What is that little kid doing out here by himself at the crack of dawn? Where are his parents?" their stares seemed to ask.

"I wish I knew!" I wanted to scream. "I don't know where my parents are or who they are." My fear mixed with the anger that was churning inside. I needed to keep it in check and concentrate on catching a ride to Los Angeles.

Then, with its headlights still on, a big rig loaded with bales of hay pulled over and stopped just down the road. I grabbed my few belongings in the old backpack and ran for my ride. "Where are you headed?" the driver yelled. I shouted back that I was going to the coast, and he waved me to hop in.

I climbed inside the cab. The big rig lurched forward and we headed for the pass through the big mountain range that seemed to loom all the way to the sky. Straight ahead lay the famous Ridge Route, my escape from this godforsaken valley. This highway would take me through these mountains to the Pacific Ocean. This highway would take me to a new life.

The big diesel engine purred as we drove across the valley. Soon the road began to wind up into the mountains. The driver was nice. He asked me questions but didn't pry into my personal life. I lied to him, telling him that I was on the way to visit my aunt and uncle who lived on the coast north of Los Angeles. He said I was very lucky because that's the area where he was going to deliver his load of hay.

He didn't seem surprised that I was hitchhiking alone. These were very tough times in California and the nation. Many people did not have the money for trains or buses. Catching a free ride by sticking out your thumb was not uncommon. Well, maybe a little unusual for a kid my age.

The smooth purr of the motor relaxed me. My eyes felt heavy. I had slept very little the night before as I planned my escape. Leaning my head back against the seat, I fell into a deep but troubled sleep.

I dreamed. How did this all begin? I tried to recall my earliest memories, all the way back to my first foster home. I remembered being in a large room with many people. I was just three years old, and there was an old man wearing a black robe sitting in front of everybody. He hit his wooden hammer down on his desk and yelled, "Next!" A woman sitting next to me took me by the arm and led me up to the man in the robe. I was frightened to death.

"What is your mother's name?" he asked me. I was scared speechless. I didn't know her name, so I just shook my head. "What is your father's name?" he demanded. Again, I didn't know the answer, so I just shook my head. The woman standing next to me called him "Judge." He looked down at me one more time. Then he picked up a pen and signed a piece of paper. In a loud voice he said, "He's a ward of the court."

The truck climbed steadily up into the mountains as I continued my dream. The lady in the courtroom drove me to a large red brick building and parked the car. She took me inside where another lady sat at a desk. She signed a piece of paper and turned to me. "You'll be safe here, Walter." After giving me a little hug, she turned and walked out the front door.

The next thing I remember, I was in a large room with ten or more boys. There were beds everywhere, and the room smelled. There were large windows, but all of them were closed off with iron bars.

The boys were much bigger and older than I, which made me feel so small. The biggest boy eyed me suspiciously. "What's this little kid doing here?" he said. I was so frightened that my legs were shaking. Some of the boys were looking out the barred windows, while others sat on the beds and talked.

"Look at this little dwarf!" another boy yelled. "Wonder who dumped him?" I wanted to cry, but I clamped my mouth shut. I was so thirsty that it was hard to swallow. I couldn't remember the last time I'd had anything to drink.

"Could I have some water, please?" I managed to mutter.

"Hey! You heard the little guy. He's thirsty. Get him some water," the biggest boy yelled.

Two boys left the room and returned with an old tin cup and handed it to me. Without hesitation, I lifted the cup to my lips and drank desperately. I was so thirsty. After the first two swallows, I dropped the cup on the concrete floor and it landed with a loud crash. While gagging, I spit out the warm liquid. All of the boys were pointing at me and whooping and laughing.

Somewhere inside my three-year-old brain, a little voice was saying, "Welcome to juvenile hall, little ward of the court! Did you enjoy your refreshing drink of pee?"

Did You Know?

- There are 75,000 kids living in California foster homes, so if you happen to live in one, you've got lots of company.

- Most foster homes are very good with caring foster parents, but occasionally one will show up where people really only want the money they receive for housing children.

- One of the biggest problems that foster home kids face is a lack of permanency. They are sometimes forced to move frequently from home to home.

- Kids living in foster homes must work to develop a positive attitude and make courage their constant companion.

Two

A PLACE CALLED SEA VIEW

The truck hit a rut in the road. My head jerked forward and I awoke from a deep and fitful sleep. "You were one tired little guy!" the friendly driver commented.

"Where are we?"

"We're down out of the mountains, and we'll be on the coast soon," he replied.

He told me that the first little town we'd come to on the ocean was Sea View.

Ocean! Can you believe I'm going to see the Pacific Ocean? I marveled. I'd seen pictures of it at school the year we'd studied California. I recalled the photographs of the beautiful waves crashing and rolling up on the white sandy beaches. What a far cry from the little dry farm belt where I had been living for the past few months!

"You'll have to tell me where you want to get off," the driver said. "At Sea View, I'm going to turn off the coast and head inland again. You told me your aunt and uncle lived along this coast."

"Sea View will be fine. I'll call them from there," I lied.

It was early afternoon as we drove along the beach highway heading north. My heart leaped with joy as I looked out at the endless beaches stroked by brilliant waves. The truck slowed as we entered a town with buildings covering the hillside above the beautiful Pacific.

"All off for the town of Sea View," my driver friend yelled as if he were a train conductor. "You take care of yourself, son. I hope we meet again someday."

I opened the door, climbed down on the running board, and jumped to the ground. "Thank you, sir. Thank you so much!" I said with heartfelt sincerity. I was, of course, thanking him for the ride, but in a way, I may have also been thanking him for calling me "son." No one had ever called me that before.

The big rig pulled away as I waved good-bye. Turning, I looked up the street and saw small office buildings on one side and a row of old houses on the other. The afternoon breeze was crisp and smelled of the sea. The scent was a breathtaking sensation, one I had never experienced before. I had only dreamed of coming to the sea. I had no idea that it had it's own special fragrance.

The sign on the post next to me said "Oak Street." I was looking up Oak Street at the foothills overlooking the ocean in a town called Sea View. Everything about this place appeared perfect. It was like a picture you might see on a postcard, only postcards don't have a fresh smell.

Throwing my old tattered backpack over my shoulder, I walked up the short street. I needed to find some place to stay before nightfall. There was little traffic, and the town seemed quiet. Walking past two or three old two-story homes, I stopped abruptly in the middle of the block. I was standing in front of an old brown house with a sign in the front window. It read, "Room for rent."

Is this possible? I asked myself. I needed to find a place, but this was too good to be true. The very first street I walked in Sea View, and I saw a sign about a room for rent. Who knew what rooms rented for on the coast? In my pocket was

$38.13 in old one-dollar bills and change, which I had earned, hidden, and saved over the past year. Could I possibly afford a room? *There's only one way to find out,* a voice told me.

The voice sounded like Mrs. Jenkins, my fourth grade teacher in Bakersfield. "You have to trust yourself, Walter," she used to encourage me. "If you don't believe in yourself, no one else will." The support Mrs. Jenkins gave me at school helped me survive many terrible nights in some of the foster homes I had lived in.

Taking in a deep breath, I walked up the sidewalk to the front porch of the old brown house. Standing straight and bravely, I knocked on the screen door. "Just a minute," a female voice cried. "I'll be right there." An elderly lady with grey hair opened the door. She looked at me and smiled. "Can I help you, son?"

A good feeling rushed through my body. Her voice was warm and friendly. It was not Mrs. Jenkins's voice, but it put me at ease. "Hello, Ma'am. My name is Walter. I saw your sign in the window," I said politely.

"Yes, I have a room for rent. Were you looking for one?" she asked. I nodded my head, and she smiled warmly again. "Do you want it for yourself and maybe a member of your family?" she asked.

"Yes, Ma'am. My mother is coming into town tomorrow," I fibbed. "I got here early, and we need a place to stay for a while."

"I'm Mrs. Bishop, Walter. Come on in. Let me show you the room," she said, opening the screen door for me. "It's a large room at the back of the house. It's nice and quiet, away from the street. It rents for twenty dollars a month."

My heart raced with joy. I had enough money for the first month. I could earn more while I lived there. *She is such a nice lady,* I thought. *I hope she believes my story about my mother coming to town.*

The room was the most beautiful thing I had ever seen. Over the years I had lived in rooms the size of closets, slept in cold and dirty garages, and even outside in a backyard. But wow, this room was good enough for a palace! It had two beds, large windows (without bars), and a small cooking area in one corner.

There was a sink with hot and cold running water, a refrigerator, and a two-burner "hot plate" stove to cook on. On the lovely hardwood floor, there was a beautiful area rug, and it was clean! Mrs. Bishop could easily see the expression of amazement on my face. "Do you like it?" she asked with a warm smile.

I paused, searching for words, then I answered, "Oh yes, I really like it!"

She asked me if I wanted to wait until tomorrow when my mother could pay the rent. I told her no, that she had given me money in case I found the right place. Smiling from ear to ear, I reached into my pocket and pulled out the roll of old one dollar bills with the rubber band around them. I sat down at the small eating table, counted out twenty bills, and handed them to my new landlady.

Mrs. Bishop said she would be right back, and she left the room, returning shortly with a piece of paper. Handing it to me she stated, "Here's a receipt for you and your mother to keep for your records. I'll leave you alone now, Walter, so you can look around your new home and maybe unpack. Welcome to Sea View!" she added as she walked out, closing the door behind her.

All alone, I sat down on the bed. I gazed up at the high ceiling and tall windows in absolute silence. I was almost too stunned to even think. Never, in my short life, had I ever seen a place like this, let alone thought about living in it.

Outside my door was a bathroom with a toilet, bathtub, and shower that Mrs. Bishop had shown me. When I finally came to my senses, I went in and took a long, hot shower. *This is how kings live*, I thought. The little shower at the farmhouse only had cold water. This was real luxury, indeed!

Returning to my gorgeous room, I changed into my only other clean shirt and pair of jeans. *I'll wash out these dirty ones tomorrow*, I planned. There was a knock on the door, and I opened it. Mrs. Bishop was standing there with a tray. On it was a large bowl of hot soup and a lovely sandwich. To top off my surprise welcome meal, there was a chocolate chip cookie and a large glass of milk.

"I thought you might be hungry after your long day," she said. I gave her my heartfelt thanks as she walked out and closed the door. Eating silently at my little table, I slowly ate one of the best meals of my life. When finished, I climbed up on my beautiful soft bed and within seconds fell into a deep, untroubled sleep.

Did You Know?

- Students who live in tough home situations must learn to reach out to their teachers and counselors for help.

- With the support they get from school, kids can learn how to trust and believe in themselves.

- Some students live in homes where no one has graduated from high school or college. They may have to seek extra guidance and counseling.

- Some kids may live with a single relative or working adult who has little time to help them. These students should look for extra support at school.

Three

TO TELL THE TRUTH

It was probably the birds chirping outside my window that woke me up. I rubbed my eyes in amazement as I saw the bright sunlight streaming through the curtains. Had I slept through the late afternoon and all through the night? Apparently, I had. What in the world made me sleep so long? Was it the wonderful, filling meal that Mrs. Bishop made me, or the first warm shower that I'd taken in months? Whatever it was, I couldn't remember when I had felt more rested and alive.

After washing up in the bathroom down the hall, I gave my dirty clothes from the trip a good scrubbing and hung them over a wooden chair. In my little refrigerator, I retrieved the half sandwich and glass of milk left over from my welcome meal. As I ate this wonderful breakfast, I planned what I must do next.

Looking for a job had to be the first item on my list. I had given Mrs. Bishop twenty dollars yesterday. That would take care of my room for one month, but then what?

Sometimes my fourth grade teacher, Mrs. Jenkins, would keep me after school for a few minutes. She called these short sessions "setting goals," which to me meant planning for the future. At first, she had me thoroughly understand that I must trust myself if I were to succeed in life. She knew that I lived in a tough foster home and that school was the only place I felt safe. She was also aware that I awoke each day waiting for the sun to come up so I could run to school and be among friends and teachers who would "watch my back," as some of the guys would say.

During one of our sessions, we talked at length about "truth." She told me truth meant different things to different people. "There's one kind of truth among thieves and criminals," she said. "Sometimes people tell lies if they have something to gain from doing so, or if they fear the consequences if the real facts come out.

"You are a bright and hardworking boy, Walter. The truth is your friend, and it is absolutely necessary for success in life. Half truths don't last. They will catch up with a person sooner or later."

This teacher was a fine person whom I considered a friend. She didn't have to spend her valuable time with me after school, but she did. "You are a very special person, Walter. I know your home life is difficult, and sometimes it might seem to be to your advantage to tell a fib or a lie. But even bad people sooner or later will have to respect you for sticking to your guns and telling the truth."

My thoughts shifted from Mrs. Jenkins to a past experience involving telling the truth. I was in kindergarten and I lived with my first foster family. Life was not easy with them, and they punished me for any reason they could think of.

Walking home every day, I had to cross a meadow with a creek running through it. There was a small footbridge over the streambed that all the kids used.

As I approached the bridge that day, I noticed two older boys standing in the middle of the bridge, laughing. As I got closer, I noticed they were holding a thin rope or cord while dangling the other end into the water.

As I passed them, I was horrified to see a small kitten at the other end of the cord. The big boys were dangling it in the water, first letting it sink beneath the surface while struggling for its life, then bringing it up again to taunt it. The cat was petrified as it swung on the end of the cord waiting for them to drop it into the water again. The little guy fought bravely, but it was slowly going to die.

Without even a thought, I threw myself at the cruel kids knocking one of the boys off balance so that he fell off the bridge into the water. The other boy dropped the cord that was wrapped around the kitten's neck and turned on me. "You little jerk! I'm going to kill you!" he screamed. I hung on to one of his legs as he began to beat me around my head and back. Finally we, too, fell off the bridge and into the cold stream.

In the stream bed, the boy continued to pound me, but luckily for me the other kid yelled, "Leave him alone! You're going to get us in trouble!" The fight stopped and both of the older boys climbed out of the creek and went on their way. Seeing this, I got to my feet and waded to the other side of the creek where the small kitten had managed to swim. He was sitting on the bank trying his hardest to get the tight cord off from around his neck.

Picking the little wet fellow up in my arms, I gently removed the cord, petted him and put him on the ground. He shook himself briefly, then took off running across the open field toward home, I hoped.

I was a mess. My shirt was torn and I was sopping wet. Blood flowed from my nose and there was a cut on my arm from my fall into the rocky streambed. The thought of going home to my foster parents nearly threw me into a panic. There would be trouble tonight. I thought about what kind of a story to tell them.

That afternoon, the husband and wife confronted me.

What should I tell them, I thought. *I was hit by a car? A gang of kids had thrown me off of the creek bridge?* Without coaching, I decided to tell them what actually happened in detail. As I talked, I waited for the expected, "Go to your room! Look, you've ruined your only good shirt. There's no dinner for you tonight!"

I had told them exactly what had happened. I had told them the truth. But to my astonishment, nothing happened. Were they impressed that I had saved the life of a young kitten? I'll never know. They simply shook their heads, got up, and walked out of the room.

My thoughts returned to the here and now. I'd finished the half sandwich; it was time to get a move on. I loved walking up Oak Street past the old houses. A block ahead, I could see Main Street, where many of the local businesses were located, according to Mrs. Bishop. Turning the corner, I looked up the street at the shops and offices. On my right was a barbershop with a candy cane pole turning cheerfully at its front door. Next door was a restaurant. "Bill's Place," the big sign in front spelled out.

Stopping in front of the eatery, I looked inside. There were maybe twenty tables, and waitresses were scurrying everywhere. The customers appeared to be happy and were enjoying their meals. Why not? I've got to start somewhere, I reckoned.

"May I help you?" a short lady asked me, smiling. I told her I was looking for a job. "Just a minute, I'll get the owner for you," she said, walking away.

"Yes sir, what can I do for you, young man?"

Bill was middle aged. He was tall and heavy, but he looked like a friendly giant. I told him I was looking for work. He looked me over as if he wondered how strong I was.

"Come with me," he said, and I followed him into a back

room. "What kind of work are you looking for, son?"

I told him I could clean off tables and that I was an experienced dishwasher, which I was, in a way. Bill asked me if I could scrub pots and pans, and I replied that I could. I added that I lived just around the corner, and that I would never be late for work.

Outside the restaurant, I let out a loud cheer and jumped in the air. Bill had said, "Okay, let's give it a try. I need a bus boy to clear tables and someone to wash pots and pans. You'll come in after school and work the dinner hour from four to nine o'clock. You'll earn 35 cents an hour, and you'll get a free meal. How does that sound?" I beamed as we shook hands and I headed for the door.

The old houses on Oak Street flashed by as I ran home at full speed. Bursting through the front door, I was greeted by Mrs. Bishop. She could see the joy and elation on my face as I related my meeting with Bill and my new job at the restaurant. She smiled as I talked. When I finished she said, "I'm very proud of you, Walter."

My joy was short-lived when the little voice inside my head said, "The truth, Walter." I sucked in a big breath and explained to her that I had fibbed and that my mother was not arriving that day. In fact, I had never had a mother, or father, for that matter.

I told her about the truck ride across the mountains. She learned about the old farmer and his cruel wife and the many foster homes—some good, many bad—that I had endured. "I'm sorry I lied to you, Mrs. Bishop. That was not right. You are a very nice person, and if you want me to leave, I will."

There was a tear in her eye as the sweet, grey haired lady took me into her arms and said, "I thought maybe you were an orphan, Walter. But I can tell you are a very special orphan. If you want to stay and pay your rent every month like my other four renters, you are most welcome. You just live by the house rules and find yourself a school to attend. If anybody asks me about you, I don't know a thing. We'll get along just fine."

I fought back tears as I thanked her and then went to my room where I cried uncontrollably. Later in the afternoon I walked to the beach two blocks down the street. Sitting down on a high sand dune, I looked out at the magical ocean scene as the orange sun sank in the west. A cool breeze kissed my cheeks, and I felt as though I was frozen in time. In that blissful moment, I thought, *I'm the luckiest kid in the world.*

Did You Know?

- Good foster parents can provide support and a stable family for youngsters.

- California has over 13,000 licensed foster homes. The average stay for a child in a foster home is just over three years.

- Social workers try very hard to find foster homes that will provide safety and permanency for youngsters.

- Learning to tell the truth is an essential building block of a person's character.

Four

SCHOOL DAYS ARE COMING

The small grocery store around the corner had anything you could want, and it was close to my new residence. I walked its aisles, dropping a loaf of bread, a jar of peanut butter, a box of cereal, and a quart of milk in my shopping basket. It's what people call a mom and pop store, because such a store is often run by a married couple.

The man at the cash register was whistling a lively tune, and he smiled at me when I set my little basket of groceries on the counter.

"Beautiful day out there! Will this be it?" he asked. I nodded that I had everything and wondered about his strange accent. "I can tell ye haven't heard a Scotsman speak before, have ye, yank?" I told him I hadn't, and he continued, "Well, the missus and me have owned this little store for twenty years. We love our adopted country, but this crazy accent just keeps hanging on, and after awhile, people get used to it," he added, putting my purchases in a paper bag.

"My handle is Mr. Donavon," he said, holding out his hand and smiling. We shook hands, and I replied, "I'm Walter, and we have just moved into the neighborhood."

"Well, a great big welcome, Walter. Please let me or the missus know if there's anything we can do for ye. We have the best customers in the world, and we always take good care of 'em."

"Thank you, sir," I said and then added, "Oh, Mr. Donavon, do you know if there's a middle school anywhere near?"

"Indeed there is. Everything is close in Sea View. Just walk down Oak till ye get to Santa Clara. Turn left there, and the school is about ten blocks up. Ye can't miss it."

I thanked him and walked the short distance back to my house. I unloaded my purchases and put the milk in the little refrigerator, and the bread and peanut butter in the cupboard. I marveled at how well Mrs. Bishop had furnished my room. There were four of everything: four plates, four cereal bowls, four glasses, four forks and spoons, and so on. There were even four dish towels folded neatly and tucked into one of the drawers. She had thought of everything.

The grocery man was right. It was a beautiful day. Walking down Oak Street, I could smell the fragrance the ocean produced as waves rolled gently up its sandy beaches. Turning up Santa Clara Street, I headed for what I hoped would be my new school.

After an easy fifteen-minute walk, I spotted a number of red brick buildings ahead. As I entered the campus, I saw a football field and grandstands on the right. Nearby, there were other grassy areas, including several basketball courts where some boys were shooting hoops. I stopped and asked them if the office was open and one boy said it was. "Mrs. Rogers is the only one there. She's the school secretary," he added.

I knew summer was drawing to a close, because it was September. I asked them when school was scheduled to open. "Next Monday," another boy yelled. "We've only got five lousy days of vacation left and then back to the grind."

I thanked them and walked toward the building with

the office sign hanging above the door. A grind? I had never considered school a grind. School was the bright spot in a kid's life, I'd always thought. It was the one part of your life that you could really count on. Monday through Friday, school was open and there for the kids. We had the same teachers, the same custodians, and the same office workers. We knew their names and they knew ours.

My school and its teachers had been the only permanent thing in my life. Sometimes they'd change my foster home as quick as you could change a dirty shirt. There would be a knock on the door and a lady would come in and say, "Come on, Walter, it's time to go."

"Can I help you?" the woman behind the desk asked. Inside the school office, I removed my baseball cap like Mrs. Jenkins had taught me in the fourth grade. I told her my name and then repeated to Mrs. Rogers my story about moving to town. I told her I was currently staying with friends and that my mother would be arriving next week. Using her name, I politely asked Mrs. Rogers if I could have the necessary enrollment papers to take home for my mom to fill out.

The school secretary seemed surprised and pleased that I knew her name. She paused, studying me closely then said, "I suppose so. We usually don't give these forms out to new students to take home, Walter, but I'm going to make an exception for you." I thanked her for her kindness and then backed out the door, waving good-bye as I put on my ball cap.

Walking home, I glanced at the papers in my hands. *Thank goodness I'm a good reader*, I thought. Even so, I could tell that I might need a dictionary for a couple of these words.

I stopped at the beach at the foot of Oak Street. Sitting on a bench, I read the papers that would be my ticket to the seventh and eighth grades of my new middle school. Noticing the sun moving lower in the sky, I remembered where I needed to go this afternoon. Bill's Place. Today would be my first day as a professional restaurant environment engineer—or dishwasher, to use a local expression.

The popular restaurant was humming, and every table was taken. The waitresses moved quickly and efficiently while chatting with their friendly customers. I was ten minutes early, another lesson learned from a great teacher.

"Always be early, Walter, or at least on time. Tardiness shows a lack of interest, a lack of caring about the people you are keeping waiting. Promptness shows you are a real go-getter, a winner!" she had said.

I smiled at the ladies serving tables as I walked through the dining room toward the kitchen. Big Bill greeted me and handed me a white apron. He showed me how to stack dishes and glassware in the dishwasher and start it by pushing a button. "It takes about twenty minutes to wash a load," he said. "While they're washing, you can hand wash pots and pans and go out in front and clear off tables and carry the dirty dishes back to the kitchen. It's not that tough, is it?" he added.

While the big dishwasher hummed smoothly, I took a plastic dish carrier out to the dining room and cleared dishes from the now empty tables. The waitresses smiled their approval at me as they served their happy diners.

Evelyn was the oldest and appeared to be the leader of the group. Irene and Connie were younger. I had learned their names by listening to customers calling out to them. There was a young girl who also waited tables, but I didn't know her name yet. Working together every day, I knew I would get to know all of them very well.

I had done the math. My job at thirty-five cents an hour would pay me about fifty-two dollars a month, plus a free dinner each day, which was really a good deal. I could choose anything I wanted to eat and as much as I wanted. If I had nothing else to eat all day long, I could get along very well on just one luscious evening feast.

These thoughts were running through my mind when Bill yelled, "It's time to go home, everybody. Good work, I'll see you all tomorrow!"

Stars sparkled down happily as I walked the short distance home. *Just stroll around the corner onto Oak, and this kid is home!* I thought. Back in my house I washed up and got ready for bed. Sliding between the clean sheets and onto the soft mattress, I moaned with delight. I felt like a millionaire!

In seconds, I drifted off into a deep and safe sleep. Even in slumber, my well-trained ears strained to hear any threatening sounds in the night. However, they would hear no arguing, screaming, shouting, or the sound of dishware smashing on the floor. Soon my ears, too, would learn that we were now on our own, in our own secure haven where there was no poverty, hatred, or fear.

Did You Know?

- Because of their need for money, some kids are forced to find a part-time or weekend job.

- Some students work part-time throughout their middle school, high school, and college years.

- Having a part-time job can really help students develop a sense of independence and responsibility.

- Parents and guardians must provide extra support for their student who has taken on the responsibility of part-time work.

Five

SUPPORT FROM COWORKERS

Everything was going very well at my new job. I enjoyed the work and the people. I was getting to know everyone, and the women were all nice to me. Sometimes there would be a mix-up on an order and the customer would send the dish back. If the order was maybe a steak or a hamburger, the waitress would wrap the food in aluminum foil for me to take home. "Why not?" she would say. "It's going to be thrown away anyway." Bill knew his waitresses were sending food home with the new kid, and he had no problem with it. This occasional source of extra food was a terrific help to my meager budget and growing appetite.

Evelyn, the oldest of the ladies, took me under her wing. At closing time on Saturday night, she and I were talking alone in the kitchen. I was drying the last two cooking pots while she leaned against the sink, finishing a cup of coffee. She was telling me about her life growing up.

"I was a kid off the streets, dumped when I was ten. I grew up on my own, the hard way," she said.

She took another sip of coffee. "I'm not sure I'm buying your story about your mother coming to town, Walter. You're a good kid and a hard worker, but somehow you remind me a little bit of me. If I were a betting person, I'd say you are out on your own. You don't need to say anything, but if you ever need to talk with someone, just let me know."

Evelyn was really a nice person. She was happily married with a family of her own. I could feel her motherly concern about me when I came to work every day for my five-hour shift in the kitchen.

I put down my dish towel and briefly told her how I had gotten there from the valley. I related how I could take no more of the old farmer and his abusive wife, that my entire life up to now had been a series of foster homes until the friendly truck driver brought me to the coast.

She had tears in her eyes when I finished talking, and she gave me a big hug. She was happy about my room at Mrs. Bishop's place and that it was working out so well. Once again, she let me know that she was there to help me if I ran into any problems.

"Evelyn, there is one thing that is troubling me," I told her. I explained that school was starting on Monday and I had enrollment papers that needed to be signed. I had already neatly filled out the forms with my manuscript printing that I had mastered in the third grade. My teacher had said my printing was so perfect that she wanted me to write the greetings in all of the Christmas cards the students were making for their families. That was a big job, and it took me about a week, but boy, did I remember how to print!

I told her that Mrs. Bishop and I had an agreement. Should anyone ask, she was going to say that I was just another renter. She didn't know anything about who else lived with me in my lodging. "It's none of my business who's taking care of Walter. All I know is that they pay their rent on time."

She had already done so much for me that I hated to ask her to sign my school enrollment forms. "Say no more," Evelyn said. "Tomorrow is Sunday. Bring the papers to work with you and I'll sign them. I know you haven't got a phone in your room, so we'll use my home number for you. I'll tell my husband about our deal just in case anyone calls. He's a good guy, and he'll be happy to help. By the way, I want you to come to our home for dinner the first holiday the restaurant is closed. You'll meet my kids. I think you'll like them."

She hugged me again, and we left Bill's Place. On the way home I shook my head in amazement. Where were all these wonderful people when I was growing up? I thought the only kind people in the world worked in schools, but I was wrong. There are a lot of terrific folks out there. I guess all you have to do is go out and find them.

Back in my room, I washed up and climbed into bed. The events of the day flowed through my head. I'd met so many nice people the past few days. I thought again, *where were they when I was a small child of three, six, or even ten years old living on the farm from hell?* Laying there in the darkness, my mind went back to my kindergarten days when I was an old guy of five pushing six years of age.

I was walking home alone from school that horrible day that I found a dime on the sidewalk. Why was it so terrible to find money? You'll soon find out. There was a small grocery store on the way and I was very hungry so I stopped in to see what I could buy for a dime. There were boxes of candy bars on the counter, so I gave them my dime and left. During the next few blocks of my walk home, I snacked on the delicious candy, never remembering having eaten anything so wonderful.

At dinner that night, the couple sat at their usual places at the table with their only child sitting across from me. She was a really weird eight-year-old. Her favorite game was playing "doctor," and she always had to be the doctor while I, or one of the neighbor kids, was always the patient. But that's another story.

The three of them chatted away. They hardly ever asked me anything, so I usually remained silent. However, I suppose I was happy over my good fortune when I found the dime.

"Guess what? I found a dime on the way home from school today. It was just laying there, right in the middle of the sidewalk," I added with a grin.

The room fell into a deadly silence. It was so quiet you could hear a cricket chirping softly in the backyard. "And where is the dime now, Walter?" the mother said in a whisper. I had heard her use that tone of voice before, and it always meant trouble. She had an explosive temper that usually showed itself right after she used that tiny, childlike voice.

Trying to stay calm, I could feel myself beginning to shake. "I bought a candy bar at the store," I managed to get out.

"And what did you do with the candy bar, Walter?"

I told her that I had eaten it on the way home.

"You what? If you ever find any money you bring it to me at once. You are an evil little boy!"

Jumping up from the table, she grabbed me by the arm and jerked me out of the chair while her husband glared his approval. Pushing me out the front door she said, "You'll sleep outside with the rest of the wild animals, and I hope they get you," she shrieked, slamming and locking the door.

It was December, and it was cold outside and beginning to rain. *Where can I find shelter?* I asked myself. Then I remembered the woodpile in the backyard. There was a big pile of logs, waiting to be cut into firewood. Weeks ago, some kids and I found a space in the back of the pile. We were able to crawl in under the logs and make a fort.

Finding my secret entrance, I crawled through the weeds and mud until I was near the center of the pile. Rain still found its way to my body, but not with the same force as on the outside. I curled up in the mud in my wet jeans and T-shirt, trying to find a little warmth. Lightning began flashing overhead, and the rain became heavier. Then came the thunder, ripping violently through the skies as I lay there silently shaking.

It was difficult to know how much time had passed, but after awhile the rain seemed to become softer, like background music. The sound of the thunder mellowed as it rolled softly across the night winter sky. This music of the night seemed to have a calming effect, because this little five-year-old wiped the tears from his eyes, wiggled deeper into the mud, and went to sleep.

Did You Know?

- We all need to learn to make good decisions and be responsible for ourselves.

- Students growing up often get a lot of guidance and support from both their families and friends.

- Good attendance at school at any grade level is a must for success. Being there every day with homework in hand is a winning combination.

- Statistics show that kids who drop out of school will earn about half of what a high school graduate will make, and about one-third the pay of a college graduate. It really pays, in real dollars, to stay in school.

Six

SCHOOL BELLS RING

The next day I jumped out of bed early, eager for my first day at my new school.

After dressing, I poured dry cereal into a bowl and covered it with milk. I didn't add sugar, though, because years ago a teacher had told our class that sugar was bad for kids. One of my classmates had just lost a tooth at recess, so our teacher asked if she could have it. "Sure," the girl replied, taking her tooth to the front of the room.

"Watch," our teacher instructed as she placed the girl's tooth in a small bowl. We watched while she opened a bottle of cola and poured it slowly into the bowl until it was half full. "Let's check on this tooth about once a week and see what happens. This will be a nutrition lesson, kind of a science experiment," she added.

The school year passed, and the teacher had to remind us to check on the tooth. After some weeks, she pointed out spots where the enamel on the tooth was wearing away. A couple of months later, we saw pitted holes where the tooth was slowly rotting away, a victim of the evil soda, which was heavily laced with sugar.

So, no evil sugar on my cereal! Anyway, I couldn't afford to buy it!

As I walked toward my new school, I noticed that the sidewalks were not empty like the last time I made the trip. There were girls and boys everywhere, talking and laughing as they made their way toward the middle school campus. Their happy mood made me think this was going to be a fun place to learn.

By the time I arrived, there were hundreds of students standing around the edge of the school grounds, chatting in groups and waiting for the bell to ring, which would be the official signal that it was okay to come on the campus. I was told that most of the classes were located in the large, two-story brick building. The shop classes were out in back, not far from the gym and playing fields.

However, there was one important thing that happened to me on my first day in middle school. Every time the bell rang, students left the room and went on to their next class. No more sitting comfortably all day in the same classroom with the same teacher like we used to in elementary school. When the bell rang we moved, because we only had four minutes to get to our next class or we would be marked tardy.

What made it even tougher was that some of our classrooms were upstairs at the far end of the building. I knew we would learn how to make our six-period schedules on time, but right now all of this rush of movement was a bit nerve-racking.

Even with the new challenges, it was a nice first school day at Sea View. All of the teachers had seating charts, but they called out our names so we got a chance to learn the names of our fellow students.

One boy named Mike was in every one of my classes—even P.E.! Mike was tall with a nice smile, and when we realized we were always walking toward the same room together, we started talking.

Mike had lived in Sea View all of his life. He had a

mom and dad, but no siblings. After our last class, we left the campus and found that we were walking in the same direction. He lived much closer to the school, but we did walk a few blocks together.

I told Mike I lived with my mom on Oak Street and that I had a job after school. When we got to his street, he turned off and waved good-bye. "Maybe you could stop by my house some day after school and shoot a few hoops!" he yelled as he waved good-bye.

"That would be great!" I yelled back. School was out at two o'clock, and I didn't have to be at work until four. A little one-on-one would be fun.

The day had gone by like a flash, I thought as I continued walking. I already loved Sea View Middle School. The students looked friendly and appeared to be serious about school. In one or two of my classes today there was a joker who would probably turn out to be the class clown, but that was always the case.

Anyway, I had met my first friend. That thought almost stopped me in my tracks. How long had it been since I'd had a friend or had even thought about playing a little basketball? Basketball! What fun! What a luxury!

As I continued toward Oak Street, my mind focused back to the past months on the barren farm in the valley. Back then, when I got off the school bus at the end of our dirt road, I would walk as slowly as I could, kicking clods in the dust as I moved toward the old farmhouse. Always, when I neared the place, the old woman would step out the back door and yell, "Hurry up, Walter! What are you, some kind of a snail?"

When I dumped my books inside the back door, she would yell, "Well, what are you waiting for? You need to weed the squash rows today. You can stop when it gets dark and come in for dinner," she would add. If I had my choice,

I would stay out in the field all night rather than come in and be forced to eat the spoiled vegetables she had boiled for hours.

No, there had been no basketball on the farm. It had seemed more like a prison. There had been just the weird old farmer and his wife, the warden. There had been no friends like Mike, either. The closest living things I had to talk to had been the black crows that sat on the fence posts or an occasional jack rabbit passing through, heading for greener pastures.

I shook the scowl off my face and replaced it with a smile as I approached the beach at the end of my street. I reminded myself that this was not the dusty road leading to a broken-down farmhouse. This was Oak Street, the most beautiful spot in the world. This was my home now, operated by Mrs. Bishop, my wonderful landlady and friend.

It was still early, and I had plenty of time before I had to be at work, so I veered left and went down to the beach. If there is anything that will clear one's mind of sorrow, it's the ocean. As I sat there on the beach, with pelicans floating by and seagulls screeching at one another, I listened to the sound of the waves crashing on the shore. I thought of schools and teachers from my past.

Throughout my life thus far, my teachers had been there for me. They were my road signs when I got lost. They were my cheerleaders who urged me on when things got tough at a foster home. They had comforted me with their guidance and moral support during my darkest days.

My teachers had always said, "Nothing can conquer you when you have courage and determination, Walter." Remembering those words and almost hearing those supportive voices, I jumped to my feet and raced up the street to my new life.

Did You Know?

🔖 Elementary school kids moving up into middle school might need a little time to adjust. No longer will they have just the one class and a one-teacher program, but will probably attend multiple classes.

🔖 Very often girls will be more physically developed than boys at middle school age.

🔖 Most middle school kids have ravenous appetites because they are growing so quickly.

🔖 Students going to middle school usually prefer to hang out with their peers more than students at any other grade level.

Seven

CALLED TO THE OFFICE

The first few weeks of school went okay. I liked my teachers and my classes, and I did my homework every night.

However, something wasn't quite right. In elementary school I had gotten mostly As with an occasional B. I realized that classes were harder here in middle school, but even so, now I was getting mostly Bs with a C thrown in sometimes.

I was always at school bright and early, and I hadn't missed a day since school began. So, what was happening? I understood the class material and homework, but somehow I wasn't cutting it. I expected more from myself.

When the note to me arrived from the counselor's office, I nearly panicked. *What have I done wrong?* I thought. My teacher handed me the hall pass and told me to go.

When I arrived at Mr. Malcom's office, there was another student waiting outside on the bench. She looked at me when I sat down. She had a hound dog depressed look on her face, probably exactly like mine.

"Do you know why we're here?" she asked nervously. I shook my head, letting her know that I didn't have a clue. The two of us sat and wiggled anxiously on the bench for five minutes until the counselor's door finally opened.

"Hi! I'm Mr. Malcom, the seventh grade counselor. Come in, please." He was a nice looking man, maybe a little older than the other teachers, although it was hard to guess the ages of our teachers. Anyone over the age of eighteen was ancient to us. "Sit down and make yourselves comfortable. I just wanted to chat with you for a few minutes. You're not in any kind of trouble," he added.

I felt a little weak in the knees as I pulled out the wooden chair and sat down. I had always been a good student, so I had hardly ever been to a principal's or counselor's office, unless it was to see a social worker who was concerned about my foster home.

"I called you in together because you share very similar problems. You both are bright, and with a little extra help, you could do better at school.

"For example, Carolyn, you live with your mom, alone, just the two of you. Is that correct? Tell us about your typical day when you get home from school."

Carolyn looked a little unsure. She didn't seem to know what our visit was all about, but she began to talk. "I leave school and walk home. I have my own key to the house, because Mom has already gone to work. She usually gets home after I've gone to bed."

"Are you able to do your homework and study all of that time?" Mr. Malcom inquired.

"No," Carolyn haltingly answered. "Mom is wonderful, and she works hard for us seven days a week, but I have to pitch in by doing laundry and cleaning the house. Some days I also go to the store to buy food for us. Mom can't shop, because she has to get her sleep during the day. All of this doesn't leave me much time for studies, but I do the best I can," Carolyn concluded.

"And you do very well," the counselor exclaimed. "Most kids would flunk school with that kind of workload.

"How about you, Walter? You also live with a single, working parent, don't you?"

Here come more lies, I thought. *Would there ever come the day when I could tell the whole truth to people?*

"Yes, I live with my mom and she also works a lot. I have about an hour or so to do my homework when I get home from school. I need to work too, so I have a part-time job at a restaurant. After work I get home a little after nine o'clock every night, so it doesn't leave much time to study," I managed to say.

"Well, you should be proud of yourself that you're doing as well as you are," Mr. Malcom said, smiling. "Here's the deal, guys," he added, sliding his chair closer to the table. "We have a special class here at school that is an elective. It meets every day for one period, and it is designed to give students like you an extra boost.

"Let me tell you about it. It's not for dummies. It's for bright kids like you who have special circumstances, such as living in a foster home, or perhaps with one parent, or maybe living with a relative. These are students who should be thinking about attending college.

"This class teaches students how to get organized so they can take maximum advantage of their study time. It also teaches coping skills for kids that might not have a perfect home life. A skill like learning to overcome hardships is worth its weight in gold as we go through life," he added.

"So, Carolyn, Walter, what do you think? This class can teach you both to become independent learners and to maintain positive attitudes even when things get tough. The teacher and I will send home information that will keep your moms well informed about what's going on in your class so they can support your efforts."

Carolyn and I looked at one another after our counselor finished his sales pitch. A class to teach you how to better manage your time and how to deal with some of the stuff that's going on in your life? That didn't sound half bad!

"Sounds great, Mr. Malcom" I said with sincerity. Carolyn nodded her head, indicating that she was okay with the class, but wasn't really convinced that it would teach us all of those things. *Well, we'll see*, I thought. *Time will tell.*

Walking home from school, I thought about Carolyn. She was such a nice girl and was living a life very much like mine. The only difference was that she had a mother who she saw briefly during the week.

After work, I finished my social studies report and went to bed. While I was sleeping soundly, I had a scary dream about wild animals. I remembered exactly how these wild animal nightmares had begun.

I had once lived with foster parents who had no other children. I was about seven years old. It was the middle of summer, and the nights were warm. For some reason, the husband thought it was a good idea for me to give up my little sleeping couch and move out into the large backyard among the tall trees where I would sleep on an old army cot. His wife didn't care either way, so out into the backyard I went. Not just for one or two nights, but for the entire summer.

As if it wasn't spooky enough to sleep outside all by myself in the dark with all the strange noises, one night they had friends over to see a movie. They showed the film in the backyard where I slept.

With the screen set up near my cot, I watched a cute monkey eating fruit high up in a jungle tree. The movie continued as he ate with his friends in the safety of the high trees. What the little guy didn't know or see was the giant python snake quietly sliding up the tree trunk, getting closer and closer to the diners.

Then, with one huge lunge, the snake threw himself over

the little monkey, quickly encircling his body with his giant coils. His friends fled for their lives as the constrictor began to squeeze the life out of the little guy. He waved his arms and screamed as the iron-like coils tightened around his body. Finally, the gruesome scene ended when they both fell from the tree to the ground where the giant reptile finished off his victim.

When the movie ended, the foster parents and their friends got up and went into the house for dessert. With all the lights off and the sudden quiet, the mysterious sounds of the night returned while I lay shaking with my head tucked under my pillow.

Eventually, I fell asleep. At dawn the sun rose over the backyard. Sitting up, I rubbed my eyes and was thankful that I had escaped the huge snake and had survived another night in just one more of my frightening foster homes.

Did You Know?

- School districts have worked hard to find ways to provide classes for students with special circumstances, such as those living in a foster home, or with just one parent, or a relative.

- AVID stands for "Advancement Via Individual Determination" and was developed by Mary Catherine Swenson, an English teacher in San Diego, California.

- In recent years, AVID classes have become very popular with students, parents, and teachers. More than 90 percent of AVID students go on to enroll in college.

- AVID classes are provided both in intermediate and high schools, grades 6 through 12. Some schools offer AVID classes to students starting at grade 4.

Eight

FRIENDSHIPS

If they started classes at school an hour earlier it would certainly please me. I loved everything about my new middle school and I couldn't wait to get there in the morning.

Often I would bump into my new buddy, Mike, while walking up Santa Clara Street toward the campus. He would come out of the side street where he lived and we'd walk the rest of the way together.

"Hey, how's that new class you're taking?" he inquired one morning. We walked on together and I explained that I liked it. I told him the teacher was great, and she was really getting all the kids organized.

"We do a lot of reading and a lot of writing too," I added. "I think it's really helping me make the best use of my study time after school and to focus on what really needs to be done. I guess learning skills like these are what the class is all about."

"And how's that new girlfriend I see you walking with after your 'special' class? She's cute and blonde. What's her name?"

"Her name is Carolyn. She's a nice girl, but she's not my girlfriend. She pretty much lives alone, because her mom is working all the time to support them. Carolyn does the shopping and housework as her part of the bargain. She's a hard worker, a really nice girl."

"You know, when I hear stories like hers, I feel a little ashamed," Mike admitted. I asked him why. "Because I'm really lucky. I have both a mom and a dad who take care of me. Dad has a good job, so Mom doesn't have to work outside the home. We have a pleasant and comfortable life. I guess I'm really just a spoiled brat!" Mike concluded.

"Yeah, you are!" I yelled as I took off running the last block to the campus. Mike was hot on my heels as we slowed to a walk and joined the rest of the kids waiting for the bell to ring. "Don't be upset, Mike, because you have a great home and family. Just appreciate it. Enjoy it. And when are we going to shoot some hoops?"

"How about after school today?" The bell rang as I accepted my new friend's challenge, and we walked toward our first class.

I was beginning to feel better about school. The work seemed easier, and my grades were improving. I knew I owed a lot of this newfound success to my "special" class, as Mike called it.

Mrs. Williams taught the class, and she was excellent. She always seemed to know when students were having trouble with an assignment or a class project, and she was quick to offer help.

Also, I loved the class because it wasn't boring. We weren't pounding away at reading and writing assignments every day. Sometimes we even had interesting guest speakers. Once we had a counselor from the local college, who talked to us about how important these middle school years were in getting ready for high school and then college. He was an excellent speaker and made our educational future fit together in an understandable pattern. He told us we would all be stunned at how fast these years would fly by.

Carolyn had seemed quiet during class. She was always attractive with her scrubbed clean and neat blonde appearance. However, today she appeared as though she might be down in the dumps.

As we walked to our next class together, I asked her if everything was okay. "You look great, but you seem as though you might have a load on your mind."

She thought for a moment and then replied, "Mom's not feeling well. She's missed work this past week, which isn't good. She really needs to see a doctor, but we don't have the money." Carolyn went on to say that they rented their little house on a month-to-month basis and that they couldn't afford to get behind in the rent.

I shook my head in silent sympathy as we walked. "Carolyn, where's your lunch? Usually you bring a sack lunch like mine. Did you forget it?" She shook her head and went on to tell me that they were cutting costs by skipping meals.

"My mother is a night cashier at a service station with a convenience store. The owner pays her once a week, and he's not the greatest boss in the world. He's quick to fire any employee who messes up or is absent from work too much. We're holding our breath that Mom will get well soon."

The bell rang as I told Carolyn, "I'll meet you at the outside tables at lunchtime. I made a huge lunch for myself at the restaurant last night, and there's more than enough for both of us." She started to shake her head, and I yelled, "Don't argue!"

When the lunch bell rang, I was starving. As we walked out the door of the classroom, I asked Mike if he'd do me a favor. Mike and I usually ate our sack lunches together, but when I explained about Carolyn, he immediately understood why we needed to eat separately that day. She was a super nice girl, and nobody wanted to embarrass her for having no lunch.

Carolyn was already sitting at the picnic table when I arrived, and she greeted me with a wave.

"Okay," I exclaimed, "Let's open this surprise package and see what's inside." One of the neat things about my job at Bill's Place was his generosity. He insisted that I make my school lunch before I went home at night. Bill wanted to make sure I was eating properly.

"See, I told you there was plenty," I reassured Carolyn. "We have one turkey sandwich and one meatball sandwich, which is huge! For dessert, we've got homemade apple pie like only Bill can make." I'd cut the sandwiches in half when I made them the night before, so it was an easy lunch for us to split.

Sitting there at the picnic table with Carolyn seemed to be drawing the attention of some of the kids passing by. She and I usually walked together briefly after our class, but now just the two of us dining privately? We could see that tongues were going to wag and gossip was going to fly.

Middle school kids have a lot of fun, and one of their favorite activities is the rumor mill. Who was seen with whom, who was dating whom, who just broke up, and so on. Some students can get carried away with the teasing that sometimes goes with the social gossip, but when kids start making up cruel and untrue stuff, that's going too far.

At my new school, going too far can be called harassing or bullying, which can get you suspended or, if continued, expelled from school. Our teachers and counselors tell us, "Fun is fun, and a little friendly kidding is okay, but keep it under control. If it takes on a cruel tone, then disciplinary action might be forthcoming."

Carolyn and I finished lunch, and I said, "See you later" as I headed toward my next class. She had been very generous with her thanks for sharing my sack lunch. I felt good about it, but I was worried about her mother and what might happen to this nice little family.

After school, Mike and I walked to his house and played two short games of one-on-one basketball in the driveway. Tall Mike blew me away the first game, but I managed to win the second because I am a little faster on my feet.

After our games, Mike took me into his house and introduced me to his mom. She was a nice lady with dark hair just like Mike's, but she wasn't nearly as tall as her son. "Sit down, Walter. Would you like a soft drink or some water?" She poured a glass of cola for each of us, and she sat down to talk.

She asked how long we'd lived in Sea View, and I explained that we were new to the town and had only been here for a couple of months. She inquired about brothers or sisters, and I told her that there were just the two of us, "Me and my mom."

There was piano music playing in the background. No orchestra, just a pianist performing a classical piece. I asked her if she knew what it was, and she answered, "It's a recording of Chopin's Polonaise. Isn't it beautiful?" she exclaimed. I nodded my head in an enthusiastic "yes" as I continued to listen intently. Never before had I ever heard anything so bright and moving. I decided to go to the school library to find out more about Mr. Chopin.

I thanked Mike and his mom for the cold drink and great music and made my way home. After working on my homework for a bit, I made my way up the street to Bill's Place.

Just before closing time at the restaurant, Evelyn approached me. "Hey, Walter, my man, you look like something's bothering you tonight. Am I right?"

I explained to my friendly coworker about my sack lunch with Carolyn and how Carolyn's mom was ill and unable to go to work. I told her that Carolyn was worried sick that they couldn't afford a doctor, and how her mom's boss was quick to fire people who didn't show up for work.

Evelyn is probably one of the most sympathetic and caring people in the world. She said, "Hey, I know something that might help them out. Sea View is a good town, and people here care about one another. Just off Main Street is a free clinic where you can see a doctor and pay what you can afford. If you're broke, you don't pay anything." Having said that, she reached for the phone book and wrote down the address and phone number of the clinic on a small pad. "Tell them to try this. Now let's see a smile on that face!"

The next day, I told Carolyn about my conversation with Evelyn and handed her the piece of paper Evelyn had given me. She thanked me warmly but declined to join me for lunch. After class, I saw her heading for the school office. Later, I learned that she had gotten permission to leave school early because she wasn't feeling well. I knew where she was heading. I hoped they could help her mom!

Did You Know?

🔖 It is important for students to learn to overcome hardships in their lives and to improve their coping skills.

🔖 Like other students, AVID kids may come from low-income families, foster homes, or one-parent homes.

🔖 In AVID classes, these students are helped to develop their attitudes, such as determination and resolve.

🔖 AVID classes emphasize organizational skills and good study habits. It is a privilege to be an AVID student. They are expected to maintain B grades or better.

Nine

LOOKING BACK AT
MY FIRST JOB

Growing up without a penny in one's pocket is very hard to do. It was embarrassing those first years in school when students were asked to donate a little change for a good cause or buy a T-shirt or other things that most kids could easily afford. There was never any loose change in my old torn jeans. I couldn't afford a stick of chewing gum, let alone a fancy shirt or cap with the school or team's logo on it.

I had once asked my foster parents for a quarter, just twenty-five cents so I could attend a Halloween Carnival at school. There would be all kinds of food and wild rides. The event was sponsored by the PTA to raise money for the school. When I told them that I would work for the quarter, they just looked at me with strange looks on their faces and walked out of the room.

Unable to attend the carnival the next day, I sadly walked home from school scuffing my feet. I stopped at a corner for a car to pass, and then something happened that I will never forget. At the house on the corner, a man with a canvas sack filled with magazines stood talking to a lady at her front door. "Hi, kid," he called as he walked down her front side-walk toward me. "Want to buy a magazine?"

He seemed nice and had a big smile on his face. I shook

my head no, but then a thought rushed into my mind. "Hey, mister, do you make money selling those things?" I asked.

"Yeah, I make a little money. I have routes on this side of town, and I have some older kids working for me. They go door-to-door after school or on weekends selling them. They only get a few cents for each copy they sell, but in time it adds up," he said.

He had sports and auto magazines and copies of the *Saturday Evening Post*. He had an astonished look on his face when I inquired, "Will you give me a job? Can I sell magazines for you?"

The man fought back laughter, but managed to ask, "How old are you, kid?" I told him I was six, but I knew these neighborhoods well and the people who lived here. "Where do you live?" he added. I gave him my address and pointed to my house at the end of the next block.

He studied me carefully for a full minute, probably noticing my torn jeans and old shirt. "Tell you what. I like a guy who has some guts. You look like a straight shooter, so I'm going to give you a try. Come with me."

He led me to a small pickup truck that was parked on the corner. He opened the door and pulled out a canvas bag like the one he had over his shoulder. Then he counted out twenty magazines. "What's your name, kid?"

"My name is Walter and I really need a job. I'm a hard worker. You can ask my teachers at school."

"Okay, Walter, I'm going to give you a try. You look like a nice, honest guy, so you now work for me. Every Saturday morning I'm going to come to your house and collect the money you received for selling your magazines. I'm going to give you five cents for every one you sell, which can really add up. Are your folks going to be okay with this?"

I assured him that they wouldn't object. We shook hands, and that was the beginning of a long relationship with Jake, the magazine guy. Later, I learned that most of the kids who worked for Jake were in middle school. He even had a few adults selling for him, because these were tough times and there weren't a lot of jobs.

Every Saturday morning, like clockwork, Jake knocked on the front door and we sat down on the front porch and counted out the money I owed him. It didn't take me long to learn that the *Saturday Evening Post* magazine was a favorite with women, so I did pretty well with the housewives that came to the door when they heard my knock. Soon I stopped selling the other magazines and just carried the *Post* to my lady customers, who grew in number.

During the coming months, I was very frugal with my earnings. A nickel isn't much, but if you put each one away and watch them grow, they can be worth a fair amount of money in no time.

I was happy with my little after-school sales job. I was becoming financially independent. My foster parents didn't know or care where I was, because if they were home, they were drinking. The husband had a serious alcohol problem, and his wife wasn't far behind.

In my tiny room one night, I counted out my savings and smiled when the total was $27.65. I was rich! Since I met Jake, I had worked hundreds of hours, and all of my nickels were there in the small box that I kept hidden in my closet. The next day I went to school, as usual, and returned to the house to pick up my magazines and start my route.

As I approached the front door, I could hear voices yelling out terrible words, which meant my foster parents were at it again. Normally, I would turn and leave and return after dark, but now I needed my magazines.

From the small living room, I could see the husband and wife in the kitchen shouting at each other face to face. He pushed her hard, and she fell back against the stove.

She swore at him as she turned to grab the hot coffee pot resting on the burner. Swinging it with all her might, she struck him on the head, and the coffee and coffee grounds flew everywhere.

I stood frozen with fear as I watched the violence unfold in the small kitchen. The husband had fallen to the floor after he was hit by the hot coffee pot, but now he was attempting to get to his feet. "I'm going to kill you," he shouted as he lunged for a butcher knife lying in the kitchen sink. His wife ran from the house screaming for help from the neighbors.

When the police arrived, I was sitting in the backyard crying. My tears were not about the fighting. I had witnessed their domestic violence many times before. When the wife fled the house, I had run into my bedroom to hide. While there, I checked my closet looking for the little box where I kept my life's savings. It was gone!

Suddenly it became clear to me. When I watched them fighting in the kitchen, I noticed that something was different. Usually when they got drunk, there was a cheap bottle of wine sitting on the sink. They didn't have enough money to buy hard liquor.

But tonight was different. There were two bottles of expensive alcohol sitting on the kitchen table. One was empty and the second was about half full. They had apparently purchased the best available liquor they could find. All of my hours and months of hard work talking to mothers and housewives trying to persuade them to buy the *Saturday Evening Post* had been for naught. In less time than it took me to walk home from school that day, they had poured my entire savings down their throats in the form of whiskey.

It grew dark as I sat in the backyard. The police had taken the couple away. Earlier, I had overheard one of the neighbor ladies telling the police officers about the little boy who lived with them. "He's not their son," she said. "I don't know what the arrangements are."

I knew what was about to happen as I sat there in the darkness. I was going to be moved to a new foster home. Finally, fighting back tears, I got up and went into the house and to my room. Reaching under the bed, I pulled out my old backpack and began stuffing it with my few belongings. When I finished, I walked out the front door and sat down on the step as a car pulled up and parked behind the police car sitting there.

A middle-aged lady got out, walked up to me, and said, "Walter?" I nodded. "It's time to go." I nodded yes again, got up, and walked to the car.

I was sitting on my bed in Sea View thinking about money when the old magazine salesman days flashed through my mind. Bill had paid me at the restaurant the night before and had told me that he was very happy with my work. In fact, he said, "I'm going to give you a raise." How can it get any better? I had a beautiful room at Mrs. Bishop's home and the best job in town that also provided me with nearly all of the food I needed.

The memories of my days as a six-year-old magazine salesperson were still vivid; however, they were beginning to fade since I was out on my own and extremely happy with life.

Did You Know?

🖋 Youngsters suffer greatly when they are moved often, as some foster kids are when they are frequently shuffled from home to home.

🖋 43 percent of foster children are moved three or more times while growing up.

🖋 Frequent moves of foster children eliminates home support and weakens the self-confidence of these students.

🖋 Without counseling and special classes, fewer than 10 percent of foster kids enroll in college.

Ten

SURPRISE VISIT TO THE COUNSELING OFFICE

It was pouring cats and dogs as I walked to school the next day. I didn't have any rain gear, but Mrs. Bishop had loaned me an old black umbrella. As I was leaving my Oak Street home she grabbed me by the arm. "Walter, take this with you or you'll be sitting around school all day in wet clothes!"

Mrs. Bishop was a wonderful person. She never tried to tell me what to do, but I knew she was always aware of what was going on. I knew she was watching over me. There would never be a way to repay her for all she had done for me since I first arrived at her front door like somebody's lost pet. On bad days, she was my anchor, a lighthouse that illuminated the darkness showing me the way home.

As the months passed in seventh grade, I found there were other adults who cared about me—my teachers. Looking back, it's hard to tell when some of my relationships with them began. Often, it wasn't anything big, perhaps just pulling me aside for a few kind words of encouragement at the end of class. I had told no one at school, not even Carolyn and Mike, about my living conditions or where I had come from, and they were my best friends.

But somehow I thought that several of my teachers sensed more about my daily home life than they let on. I felt this when receiving an occasional pat on the back for a well done report or a "Good job, Walter," when they handed me back a test paper with a beautiful "A" written across the top. Once in awhile, one of them would even keep me after class for a brief chat offering me advice and encouragement.

These caring people managed to provide a calm and stable environment for me at school. Their classrooms projected a student-friendly atmosphere where, regardless of one's home conditions, kids could feel secure and pursue excellence.

The bell rang, and I rushed on to my next class with the old wet umbrella hanging on my arm. Carolyn waved when I entered the room. She flashed a big smile, quite unlike the last time I saw her. She looked great; Carolyn always looked great, I thought.

Mrs. Williams quickly brought the class to order. She was a fantastic teacher, and everyone loved her for her ability to get the best out of the kids in her Excel Classes. The period went by like a flash. As the bell rang, I looked at Carolyn and pointed to the lunch area. She nodded, and we all filed out of class.

Outside the brick building, we walked the short distance to a lunch table.

"Hi, Walter," Carolyn said with a wide smile. "What did you think of Excel today?"

"Mrs. Williams is unreal. I never get bored in her class." We began eating our sandwiches. "How's your mom?" I inquired.

"Thanks to you and your friend at work, she's fine." As we ate, she explained how she had gone home and walked her sick mother to the little neighborhood clinic. The doctor had given her medication for the flu, and it started helping her immediately. "She's feeling much better now, Walter, and she plans on going back to work tonight."

As we continued to eat, three boys walked by our table on their way to the basketball courts. One of the creeps made a fist with one of his hands, then brought it up to his lips and made little kissing sounds as they walked by. The other two gave a forced laugh as they walked on. The kidding had slowed down as the year progressed, but it certainly hadn't stopped.

"Hi guys!" Mike yelled as he neared our table and sat down. "Mind if I join you? I had to stay after class. My teacher is not too happy with me," he added as he unwrapped a sandwich and began to eat. "She told me that the days were flying by and we'd all be in the eighth grade soon, and that this was no time for me to slack off."

"You get good grades, Mike," Carolyn said defending him. "What does she mean by slacking off?"

Mike took a drink from his milk carton. "We do a lot of projects in that class, and there are three or four kids in there that I just do not like."

I decided to jump in. "Why don't you like them, Mike? What do they do to you?"

"There's one guy and two girls who bother me. They're close friends, and I think they live in the same neighborhood. Anyway, you know that I'm one of the taller kids in our grade, and they're always teasing me about it. 'How's the thin air up there, giraffe? Bumped into any helicopters lately?'" Mike was getting upset, and he stopped eating his lunch. "So, when the teacher assigns group projects, it seems like I always get stuck with one or all of those yo-yos!"

Mike went on to tell us that he just couldn't work with this particular threesome, and that his class project work was suffering greatly.

"During class today, the guy made another wisecrack about my height. After the bell rang, I waited for him outside the classroom door and called him over. I told him that he and his two girlfriends needed to find some other target for their teasing or there would be trouble."

The kid then asked Mike if he wanted to fight and called him "stick man." "Is that what this is all about, stick man?" he had said.

My friend told us it took all of his will power to control himself. He took a deep breath, counted to ten, and then turned and walked away.

"You might want to make an appointment with one of the counselors," Carolyn suggested. "I have friends who have had problems of one kind or another with other kids. The counselor called them in, and they all sat down and discussed what was going on."

We didn't see Mike for a couple of days until he showed up at lunch again. He had a smile on his face when he said, "Thanks for the suggestion about seeing the counselor, Carolyn. I went by the office and made the request for conflict resolution. He called us all in and we talked for an hour.

"When you get to know them, they're not bad kids. It looks like the guy has a tough home life and one of the girls lives with an elderly aunt who's never home. The three of them admitted that they were kind of down in the dumps and looking for someone to take it out on. The more they talked, the sorrier I felt for them. No wonder they came to school with a chip on their shoulders and looking for trouble.

"I don't know if we'll ever become friends, but they've realized that they have to keep their personal problems out of school and not harass or bully other students because of them," Mike concluded.

"Hey, that's neat!" I exclaimed. Mike thanked Carolyn again for her suggestion as the bell rang. We tossed our paper sacks into the trash can and quickly made our way to our next class.

Did You Know?

🖋 Middle school students tend to have more social interaction than any other age group of kids.

🖋 Some kids are so caught up in the daily social activity of school that other students refer to them as "drama queens" or "drama kings."

🖋 Middle school students can be quite sensitive to criticism and teasing by members of their peer group.

🖋 Counselors and teachers can be extremely useful in helping resolve issues among students by engaging them in conflict resolution.

Eleven

A BRUSH WITH DEATH

Sometimes you hear people say that time flies. Well, that was certainly true for my year in the seventh grade. My days were filled with attending classes, rushing back to my room on Oak Street after school to do a little homework, and then on to my job. Maybe it flew because I was so busy. I certainly wasn't bored! I had a great time at school and, though in a different setting, lots of fun at work.

I've come to the conclusion that it's the people in life who make the days fun and interesting. At school I had my buddies and friends and a number of wonderful teachers who were also my friends. At work, Bill and the ladies who served diners were just super. They were like a family to me, helping me throughout the school year.

I think Evelyn should have been a teacher instead of a waitress. She was so full of advice and wisdom about how to deal with the tough parts of life. "Nobody likes a crybaby," I heard her tell a young waitress at work. "If you stand tall and try to do the best you can, everyone around you will get on the bandwagon and try to help you." Evelyn had certainly helped me, and she was also a lifesaver for Carolyn's sick mom.

Speaking of Carolyn, she had a nice friend by the name of Virginia. One day she brought her to our lunch table where she met Mike. Soon Virginia began showing up every day, and some days Mike would walk her home from school. They made a great couple. Mike was tall and kind of quiet, while Virginia was just the opposite, vivacious and funny.

We all had other friends, but not as close as the four of us. Together we shared our problems and successes during the seventh grade. It is very comforting to have these kinds of buddies, because they help you through tough days. Everybody needs friends.

When our report cards came out, I was jubilant! Five As and one B. *Not bad*, I thought, *for a kid who hitchhiked here from a desolate farm in the valley.* It was now summer vacation, and many of my friends were going on trips with their families. No school every day? What in the world was I going to do without school?

My first Saturday of the summer was a bright, sunny day. After breakfast, I read for a little while and then decided to take a walk down to the beach. As I strolled down Oak Street in my swimsuit with a towel over my shoulder, a friendly summer breeze blew up from the beach, inviting me to go for a swim. Walking through the sand dunes, I saw a couple of kids on boogie boards and several that were already bodysurfing in the waves. It looked like so much fun. I was a bit surprised that there were no lifeguards watching over the young swimmers.

I sat down on a sand dune for a while, watching the action as the sun climbed higher in the sky and began to warm my body. When I lived over in the hot valley, I had sometimes walked to a nearby canal to cool off. These canals crisscrossed the valley everywhere. They were deep, with water that would irrigate the valley's vegetable and cotton crops. I taught myself to swim while playing in the canals.

I thought about giving bodysurfing a try. Why not? Running through the shallow foamy wake, I judged the timing of an approaching wave and dove under it like I had seen the other boys do that morning. Now, standing waist deep in salt water, I watched closely as the other surfers caught and rode incoming waves. *What fun*, I thought.

It took me a half-dozen tries before I got the drift of how to do it. What an amazing thrill! Watch a big swell approaching and forming into a wave, and then swim for your life to catch it and experience the breathtaking drop as it propels you toward the shore.

I rode the beautiful Pacific Ocean waves for about an hour. They seemed to be getting larger, and I was tired and thinking seriously about getting out. There were many swimmers in the water now, most of them young, but I also noticed an older couple standing not far from me.

The couple yelled out a happy warning as a very large wave approached. Everyone ducked under it and rose to the surface laughing. The pounding sound of the surf near the shore had been loud, but now it seemed very still. Normally, as I surfed, I would be standing in chest-deep water, but now my toes could not touch the bottom.

The other swimmers and I looked at one another with expressions indicating that we knew something was wrong. We were moving away from the beach and to the south. The figures of the sunbathers and waders on the shore were becoming smaller by the second. We were being pulled out into the open sea by a strong current. One of the adult swimmers nearby put a name to it. "Riptide!" he screamed.

Everyone did exactly the same thing. Young and old, we swam toward the shore and safety. Seagulls glided overhead as we stroked and kicked for our lives. It wasn't long before some in the group became tired, and then exhausted. "God, please help me!" the elderly man cried out.

"Hang on!" his wife pleaded. Then she suddenly gagged as her mouth filled with seawater. As we all continued to struggle, we drifted farther apart, like little dots now hundreds of yards out beyond the breaking waves. What had begun as a fun beach day was now turning into a battle for my life. The pleading wife near me called out her husband's name. Each of her cries became less audible as her mouth and throat filled with saltwater. I saw her raise her arm one more time and wave at the beach for help, and then she sank below the surface, disappearing from sight.

Like the rest of our group, I swam as steadily as possible toward the beach, not knowing that in a riptide one should relax and go with the current. This kind of current will pull a swimmer along the coastline for sometimes as much as a mile before releasing him from its grip.

I, too, was becoming exhausted. Rolling over on my back to float, I tried to preserve my arm and leg strength as much as possible. However, the ocean's surface was too choppy. Seawater was continually flooding my mouth, choking me. Like the lady near me, I was going to drown. I was sure of it.

As I listened to the waves pounding on the distant shore, I began to think about my dilemma. I needed to rest from swimming so hard, but the rough ocean surface wouldn't allow me to float on my back. So, what other options did I have? *Swim on my side!*

I had never tried doing that before, but I was getting desperate. Rolling over on my side, I began to dog paddle. Then I tried reaching out with my hands cupped, pulling them back toward me while kicking with my feet. This motion was working! I could feel myself moving through the water! After about ten minutes, a wave picked me up and dumped me into shallow water along the beach.

I was too exhausted to stand, so I coughed up saltwater and crawled through the shallow foam. Two men ran from the beach and pulled me up on the sand. As I lay there, I could see people in uniforms working on the other bodies lying along the shoreline. Some, like me, had made it. Several, unfortunately, had not.

That afternoon I dejectedly made my way to the restaurant, tired and drained of emotion. "Walter, what in the world happened to you?" Evelyn shouted when she saw me. Soon Bill took my arm and sat me down at one of the tables in the rear. All of the employees, including the cooks, gathered around as I related what had happened that afternoon at the beach.

Evelyn had only worked half of her eight-hour shift, but after hearing my story, she asked Bill if she could have the rest of the night off. She didn't have to explain to him why she wanted the time off. "Come on, Walter. Grab your sweater, we're going home."

I was still feeling kind of dopey. I was exhausted, with terrible thoughts racing around in my head about what had happened that day. "We're going to my place, and I'll feed you some hot chicken soup. It will get your circulation going again after all the time you spent in that cold seawater." I had been to Evelyn's home before and had met her husband and kids. What a great and generous family they were.

After dinner and again relating my surfing tale to her family, I stood and said, "It's time for me to go. Mrs. Bishop is going to be worried."

"Not so fast, bucko!" Evelyn exclaimed. "You're not going anywhere. You're staying right here with us tonight to make sure that you're okay. I phoned Mrs. Bishop and told her you were sleeping over."

I slept alone in one of the kids' rooms. Her eldest son had kindly given up his bed. Sleep came in just minutes, but it was not a peaceful sleep. I dreamed I was floating facedown above a sunken cemetery. It was located about ten feet underwater, resting on the ocean floor. As I drifted across the graveyard, I could see grave markers everywhere covered with barnacles. In the shifting underwater light, an occasional hand would float out from behind a gravestone and beckon me to come down.

Days later I truly grasped just how kind Evelyn and her family had been. She had taken a dazed kid after a terrible experience and had given him a warm home and the comfort he needed to heal. There are times in everyone's life when being tough is just not enough. Being grateful and accepting help is a much smarter way to go.

The ocean had taught me an unforgettable lesson in my near-drowning experience. It pointed out that life is full of strong tides that sometimes try to pull us into making bad decisions. There are times when we have to swim hard against the current just to stay in school. Perhaps there are other occasions when you're tempted to fall in with the wrong crowd.

So just remember what the ocean has taught us. If you're ever caught in one of these negative tides, don't panic. Be calm and determined and make your way to the safety of the shore.

Did You Know?

- Life can offer many physical obstacles. A positive "I can" attitude, along with determination, can do much to help us overcome most of them.

- Doubting you can make it is the first step to losing. There is always something you can do.

- Seeking help is something you can always do. We can ask for help from our parents and friends, our neighbors, and our teachers at school.

- The fear of failure can be strong in all of us at times. It is important to learn that fear is a human emotion that can be overcome by maintaining a positive outlook on life.

Twelve

THE LONG DAYS OF SUMMER

After my wild battle with the riptide down at the beach, I decided to do something about it. I had read in the newspaper that the Red Cross was conducting swimming classes at the high school pool, and they were free. School was on summer recess, and I had plenty of time on my hands, so why not? Yes, I knew how to swim, but not well enough to take on the big ocean down the street when it wanted to play rough.

I began my daily lessons in the intermediate class with other kids who knew how to swim but weren't strong swimmers. In the following weeks, I completed that class and also the advanced group, ending up being able to do four different strokes pretty well. All in all, I was happy with what the Red Cross instructors had taught me about water safety and delighted that I would now feel more comfortable in any water activity.

Business was going great at Bill's Place with the town folks filling the restaurant every night in search of good food. My evenings working there were fun and busy, and the time always flew by. Every night at closing, I would sit down to a big meal with dessert and then pack up some sandwiches to take home for the next day. I guess I was eating well, because I was growing pretty fast and putting on weight.

However, as the summer days passed quietly and peacefully by, I missed school and the kids. I decided I had too much spare time on my hands. The days felt too long. What I needed was another job to make them pass faster. I didn't want another restaurant job, so what else could I do?

Mrs. Bishop was sweeping off the front porch as I left one day. "Where are you off to, Walter?" She knew I wasn't headed for the beach since I had no swimsuit or beach towel with me.

"Nowhere special, Mrs. Bishop. I'm just going to walk around town and check out the possibility of getting another part-time job. Be back in an hour or so," I added as I waved good-bye.

There was a movie theater a couple of blocks away. It had a sign in the window "Usher Wanted," but the hours posted indicated that it was another night job, and I already had one of those. On one of the back streets, I walked past a small shop with another sign posted, "Turner Wanted." I had no idea what a turner was, but I decided to check it out.

"Can I help you, young man?" the owner inquired. I pointed to the sign in the window and asked if the position had already been filled. "Nope, still open. You looking for part-time work?"

I explained to the gentleman in overalls and wearing a baseball cap that I was. I told him about my night work at Bill's Place and that he could phone them if he needed references. "Sir," I asked, "What is a turner?"

"This is a small glove factory," he explained. "We have a half-dozen ladies making work gloves on sewing machines in the back of the shop. Then the gloves go to another room where four people turn them. Each workstation has a set of metal hands with fingers that are attached to a machine. The turners put the new gloves that are sewn inside-out on the hands. With a strong pulling motion, they turn them right-side out so that the sewing stitches are on the inside where they belong.

"Sounds complicated, doesn't it?" he added. "Come on. I'll show you." He led me to a large room where three older boys were standing in front of the glove machines. We watched as they did the finishing touches on the work gloves. It looked like heavy work, and perspiration glistened on their faces.

"Think you can handle that?" he asked. My arms and upper body strength were pretty good after lifting heavy trays of plates and dishes at the restaurant, not to mention the huge iron pots and pans. I'd also developed strength from my swimming lessons. "If you want, we'll give it a try for a week to see if you can handle the heavy turning. You'll work from 8 a.m. to noon, Monday through Friday, if it works out. What do you think?"

"Yes, Sir!" I replied with a big smile. "This is certainly different from the restaurant, and I'd love to try it."

"Okay, be here tomorrow morning at eight sharp. By the way, my name is Ted. What's yours?" I told him it was Walter. We shook hands and I walked out the door.

What have I gotten myself into? I thought as I walked home from my first day at the glove factory. I was wet with sweat, and my entire body ached from tugging at the heavy leather gloves. Back in my room, I grabbed a change of clothes and headed down the hall for a hot shower.

As the days passed, however, I eventually got used to the heavy labor, and my muscles developed from the strenuous work. I knew that my "Turner" job was only for the summer, but it paid better than the restaurant, and I could save money for clothes and school supplies.

Mickey and Keith also turned gloves part time at the factory. They both claimed to be high school seniors, but they liked to goof off a lot. As the days passed, they began to talk to me more, and I soon learned that they both had dropped out of school. They liked to brag about how tough they were and called themselves "wise guys" like the hoods in the gangster movies.

One day Keith yelled at me from his workstation. "Hey, Walter! We're going out cruising tonight. Want to come along?" One thing was certain, they both always seemed to have a lot of money on them, or as they called it, folding money. Each had a roll of bills in their pockets, and they weren't one-dollar bills, either.

I thanked the guys but told them I had to work at the restaurant, which was true. When I left the factory at noon, they said, "Catch you next time, man!" I waved good-bye as I headed for home.

The following week at work, Keith and Mickey asked me to go cruising again. When I said I had to work, Keith said, "Why don't you quit that little restaurant job, Walt? You can make more dough by cruising with us one night than you can make at that dump all week."

"It's easy, man," Mickey chimed in. "We've got a friend who owns an auto shop where they sell used car parts to people. He makes a bunch of dough." He went on to explain how the two of them drove around the back streets late at night in Mickey's old pickup truck. When they spotted a nice car with a good set of chrome hubcaps, they'd pop them off with a screwdriver and stick them under a canvas in the back of the truck. "The whole heist doesn't take more than one minute," Keith bragged.

As the days passed, the two school dropouts continued to brag about how many cars they had ripped off the night before, and then they would flash their wads of bills. They continued to ask me to join them, but I always had an excuse as to why I couldn't. Finally, they gave up asking me.

I remember it well. It was a Friday morning at the glove factory. Ted, the owner, had been in earlier to talk to Keith and Mickey. He had warned them that if they didn't stop joking around and start doing more work, he was going to let them go. As he walked out the door, the two boys made faces at Ted behind his back.

Then, just before noon, two uniformed police officers walked into the shop. We immediately stopped turning gloves as they walked toward us.

"Who owns the old pickup truck parked out on the back lot?" one officer inquired. The room was so silent that you could hear a pin drop.

The other policeman said, "Well, I guess no one owns the truck. You two boys, empty out your pockets," pointing at Mickey and Keith.

"What for?" Mickey asked with a smirk on his face. But when the policeman moved toward him showing he meant business, both boys dumped everything out of their pockets onto the shop floor.

The officers looked down at the rolls of bills lying on the floor. One of them bent over and picked up a set of keys. He walked out of the shop but was back in no time. As he walked back through the door, he was pulling out handcuffs. "Looks like we found the owner of the pickup," he said to his partner. "Seems you boys have been busy in the auto parts business lately. We have your friend who buys your hubcaps down at the station waiting for you."

Keith and Mickey never looked at me as they were led out the door with their hands cuffed behind them. Their heads hung down like the defeated criminals they were.

I continued working at the glove factory until school

started. The owner was a good guy, and he asked me to come back the next summer and work for him. "We need workers like you, Walter. Stay in school, and you'll always be a winner and not end up like those two punks."

We shook hands like two good friends, and then Ted gave me a big bear hug. "I'm going to miss you, son. Stop by and see us when you have the time."

Did You Know?

- Many of the thefts committed in this country are by boys in their late teens.

- While growing up, both boys and girls might encounter gang members who want to recruit them.

- Many gang members have experienced failure and dropped out of school.

- Teens who make the mistake of dropping out of school will learn that jobs are tough to find. In fact, dropouts have a 50 percent unemployment rate.

Thirteen

A RIDE TO REMEMBER

I saw Mike a few times during the summer break from school. Sometimes we went to the beach to surf or just hang out. One thing I didn't know before living in Sea View was that beach towns get a lot of fog in the summer. It was kind of strange on foggy days to see tourists lying on blankets in the white sand, fully clothed and wearing heavy jackets. Oh well, at least they were breathing the fresh ocean air.

When we got together at Mike's house, we usually played hoops, a little one-on-one stuff. His mom would make us lunch, which we enjoyed at a picnic table in their beautiful backyard. Sometimes Mike would give Virginia a call, and she and her mom would pop over and join us. The mothers seemed to like each other a lot, they chatted and laughed while they were putting the food on the table.

I only saw Carolyn a couple of times during the break. She had a full-time job all summer babysitting a neighbor's young daughter during the day. I, of course, worked at the glove factory in the morning and the restaurant at night. Between our jobs, getting together was tough. On one occasion, she and her mom came by the restaurant so her mother could meet me. Big Bill, the owner, invited them to stay as his guests for dinner. It was a weeknight, and we weren't too busy, so I got to chat with them a lot.

However, there was one weekend when the four of us managed to get together. A big carnival had come to town, so we met down at the local fairgrounds. We walked the midway for a couple of hours, throwing baseballs at lead bottles, riding the Ferris wheel, and enjoying the hammer ride. I was lucky at a basketball throw game and won a cute teddy bear for Carolyn.

When we had enough of all the cotton candy, fun, and games, Virginia said, "Come on guys. Let's go over to the racetrack and see my dad's new horse." She went on to explain that there would be horse racing later in the day, and her dad was entering a couple of his quarter horses. "It's not far," she said, "just on the other side of the carnival near the beach."

It was a quick, ten-minute walk for the four of us, and we chatted while music from the midway blasted in the background. Soon we came across row after row of stables. "These are the stalls where the horses are kept," Virginia informed us. "There's my dad down at the end of the street," she said pointing.

Virginia's dad greeted us warmly and offered to show us his racehorses. As he was explaining the different kinds of races that would take place, a man down the street yelled at him, "He's ready, sir. Can you send one of the kids down to get him? I have another one on my hands here, and he's causing trouble."

"Okay," her father yelled back. Turning to us, he said, "Virginia, horses spook you, so you can't bring Tyrant down here. How about one of you boys? Walter, you look like you can lead a racehorse. Will you go grab Tyrant by the reins and walk him down here?"

I felt a lump in my throat, but I answered, "Sure, no problem." Over in the valley I had been around pigs, cows, and occasionally a mean chicken, but I had never been near especially a huge, strong quarter horse. However, I didn to appear scared in front of Carolyn and the others, so slowly down the little alley where Tyrant waited.

The man holding the racehorse was dressed like a jockey. When I got there, he said, "Here, son, take him by the reins." I took hold of the leather straps that hung down from the horse's head and began to lead him down the lane. "No, he doesn't seem to like being led. Here, climb on board. He's used to being ridden," the jockey said.

I'm sure my face showed fear and amazement upon hearing those words. "Don't worry, he's not mean," the jockey assured me. With that, he told me to put my foot in the stirrup that was hanging down from the saddle. I swung my leg up as high as I could and stuck my foot into the metal stirrup. The jockey gave me a boost, and all of a sudden I was up, high in the air, on a racehorse called Tyrant.

Tyrant took about three steps forward as I held the reins tightly behind his huge muscular neck. Then, without a sound, he suddenly lunged forward, and in seconds we were galloping down the little paved alley at full speed. Virginia's father screamed at the jockey, "What are you doing? Are you crazy?"

The racehorse flew down the little street running right past my friends and its owner. I, meanwhile, was hanging on for dear life. Never had I ever been so frightened! We emerged from the alley onto a main street with a lot of traffic. People frantically honked their horns as we darted in and around vehicles at a breakneck speed.

I reached down on the saddle grasping for a saddle horn that I had only seen in western movies. It was supposedly a leather knob attached to the top front of the saddle, but it wasn't there. This, apparently, was a small racing saddle, and I later learned that jockeys managed to not fall off by hanging on with just their knees. But I wasn't a jockey!

Tyrant skidded and darted through traffic for a full two minutes. We were running on the street next to the racetrack itself. Then, on the left, I spotted a wide gate in the white fence that surrounded the racetrack. It was open, and, without any guidance from me, Tyrant flew through the gate and onto the dirt track.

Once on the track, the big horse did what he was bred and trained to do. *He ran!* I held on, with my head bent low, resting on the back of his neck. I still had the reins in my hands, but they were pretty much useless. He had the other end between his teeth, and he was a lot stronger than me. Feeble commands from me like "Whoa" went unheard in the thunder of his hoofbeats. Fortunately, I had managed to squeeze my fingers under the small saddle and I hung on for dear life.

I really don't remember much about the ride, only the parts that Carolyn, Mike, Virginia, and her dad told me later. During a regular race, the horses usually only run one lap or so around the track. My friends and the animal's owner had jumped into a car and driven down to the main gate. They were standing there wide-eyed with mouths gaping in awe as Tyrant and I raced past them at full speed. They stared in disbelief as we flew down the course and into another lap.

Finally, Tyrant began to tire. He was slowing down and breathing harder with each stride. As we approached the main gate again, Virginia's dad yelled, "Pull back on the reins, son. Pull back hard!"

Hearing his command, I pulled back on the leather reins with all of my might and the big horse slowed and finally came to a stop before his owner. "Walter, are you all right?" Carolyn shouted. Virginia's dad was already out on the track.

He ran up and grabbed the reins on the horse's head as we came to a stop.

I pulled my feet out of the stirrups and slid to the ground. My legs were shaking and weak from the pounding ride. It was difficult for me to stand. Carolyn recognized my distress and held me by my arm. After a few minutes and a couple of deep breaths, I was fine and able to walk normally.

"Nice ride, Walt!" the owner yelled after he had determined that both Tyrant and I were fine. "Man, you really had the big guy rolling. You would make one heck of a jockey," he teased, ruffling my hair with his hand.

It was getting dark as the four of us kids walked back to the carnival area for cold drinks. A big moon rose above the tents and the midway.

In the distance, we could hear the loudspeakers from the racetrack. The races were about to begin. The thunder of hoofbeats filled the night air, and the announcer shouted, "They're off and running!"

I took a sip of my cola and said to Carolyn, "Man, I'm so glad they're running—without me!" She laughed, and the four of us walked to the main gate of the fairgrounds where Mike's mom was waiting to give us a ride home.

Did You Know?

- When Tyrant took Walter on the ride of his life, the horse thought they were on an exercise run.

- Horse racing has been going on for centuries. In early Roman days, chariot races were very popular.

- Some horses are called "quarter horses" because they can run full speed for one-quarter of a mile. Other racehorses can't do this.

- The first long-distance endurance race was in 1955. Horses began in Squaw Valley, California, and raced one hundred miles to the town of Auburn in Placer County.

Fourteen

MUSIC CAN LIFT OUR LIVES

Summer came to a close shortly after my brief career as a professional jockey. Mike and Virginia sometimes laughed about that fateful afternoon, but Carolyn always managed to put a positive spin on my wild ride. Carolyn and I were close friends, and she was somewhat protective and always supportive of me.

It was fun being back in school as big eighth graders. We knew the school and all of the daily routines, from classes and clubs to sports. Our newly arrived little seventh graders were busy trying to learn the ropes, and, as much as we older kids hated to admit it, they were learning fast.

All of my classes were core classes designed to prepare me for college, with the exception of one elective. Our school had a great music program that included instrument training for beginning and advanced orchestra. Chorus activities were also available for all grade levels.

During my visits to Mike's house during the summer, we had listened to different classical music selections. His mom was helpful and taught me about the various composers and their place in music history. Once in awhile, when I was feeling rich, I would buy a record from a used music store on

Main Street. These were old records, but they worked fine on Mrs. Bishop's antique player.

As summer had rolled on, I was so taken with the beautiful music of Wagner, Rachmaninoff, Bizet, and others, that I decided I would learn to play an instrument. When school started, I signed up for a class.

There was no piano in Mrs. Bishop's house, so I needed to come up with another instrument to learn. While strolling down Main Street one day, I passed an old shop with a sign stating "We sell most stringed instruments." *Maybe this is the way to go*, I thought. I loved listening to the wonderful sounds of stringed instruments. Maybe I was cut out to be a great violinist.

An elderly gentleman was working in the back of the shop. "Can I help you, young man?" he asked.

I briefly told him about the beginning instrumental classes at school, and I asked him if he had a violin I could afford.

"They run anywhere from forty-five dollars for a used one, up to five hundred for a new one," he replied.

Wow! So much for my career as a concert violinist, I thought. "Well, thank you very much, sir," I said as I turned and headed toward the door.

"Wait just a second, son. Come with me. I want to show you something." He led me to the rear of his shop where he had been working. Lying on the workbench was a beautiful new violin sitting in a black case. "I also make instruments in my spare time. This is my latest one," he said as he carefully removed it from its carrying case and handed it to me.

"You made this?" I exclaimed, truly taken with the fine polished finish on its wooden veneer. He asked me where I lived, and I told him I had a room on Oak Street. "It's amazing that you made this beautiful thing. Thank you for showing it to me."

A Boy Named Walter

When I handed the violin back, he asked me where I went to school and if my folks worked locally. I answered his questions and fibbed to him, saying there was only Mom and me in our family.

He gave me a long, pensive look. "You seem like a nice young man," the grey haired gentleman said. "I want you to have this violin. It's a gift to you as long as you play it." I'm sure my mouth dropped open. After many minutes of thanks poured out of me, I took my precious gift in its black carrying case and walked home.

In my room that night, I tried using the bow while placing my fingers at random on the strings. Nothing I played sounded like Wagner. But, then again, why should it? I'd never touched a violin before, and my music teacher would teach me.

Finally, the first day of school arrived. All of my classes were great. I was really looking forward to a super year at school. I was assigned with a group of eight kids to a beginning violin class taught by Mr. Hooper. He told us this was his first year of teaching.

During the first week, we learned to tune our instruments. Next, he taught us how to use our bows and the correct way to pull them across the strings. During those first two weeks of instruction, I felt that some of the other kids were doing much better than I. When class ended one day, two of the girls were chatting, and then they played "Twinkle, Twinkle, Little Star" together on their violins. *Wow*, I thought, *this was supposed to be a beginner's class, and they just sounded great!*

Things got worse. Mr. Hooper would say, "Let's hear G, please, class." *What is and where is "G"?* I asked myself. And, how did all the other students know how to play it? I struggled all week in that class, frantically trying to put my correct finger on the proper string to make the same sounds that the rest of the class was making.

It was easy to tell that Mr. Hooper was losing patience with me. It was also clear that I was the only true beginner enrolled in this beginner's class. On Friday, after several disappointed looks on his face, Mr. Hooper put down his baton and walked over to me. "Walter, you seem to be having a great deal of trouble. May I see your violin, please?"

I handed him the beautiful gift I'd received, and he held it up to the light. A smile formed on his face, and then he broke out in a loud laugh. All of the other kids were silently watching us. "Where in the world did you get this weird thing? I've never seen anything like it in all my life. It looks like someone made it in their garage." He chuckled again as he handed my precious instrument back to me. Just then the bell rang.

Without further comment, he walked back to his desk and sat down. The other kids looked at me as they walked to the door. From their looks, I could tell they felt sorry for me. Fighting back my bitter disappointment, I slowly put my violin in its case and followed them out the door.

That was the last day I attended Mr. Hooper's "beginner's" class. In all of my years at school I had never been so totally crushed by anyone, let alone a teacher. It was hard to fight back tears after his unkind comments. After school, I went to the counselor's office and asked for a transfer to another class—any class!

After a short discussion, the counselor transferred me to chorus, thus allowing me to drop violin and Mr. Hooper. I didn't tell her why I wanted out, but I had the feeling she knew something traumatic had happened.

On Monday, I began chorus with Mrs. Berman. There were about thirty boys and girls in my class, and I knew quite a few of them. She had already placed all of the kids in vocal range groups, so she kept me after class to test my voice. "You have a lovely voice, Walter. You're growing into the baritone range, so we'll assign you with that group of boys."

Mrs. Berman was a delightful person. She had a beautiful voice, which we enjoyed hearing when she taught us new songs. She loved opera. She taught us about the great composers: Italian, German, and French. We also learned a great deal about the various periods and schools of music.

My new chorus teacher was a welcome change. I looked forward to singing with my fellow students every day. As the year progressed, our group performed in a number of school assemblies, which was fun. At the end of the school year, we also put on a production of *Midsummer Night's Dream* for a large PTA audience. It was a packed house, and the fifteen hundred parents who attended seemed to really enjoy the show.

As time passed, I got over any resentment I felt toward Mr. Hooper for embarrassing me in front of a group of my peers. Later, I discussed the incident with Carolyn, Mike, and Virginia at lunch. We all agreed that Mr. Hooper should have talked with me privately if he had a problem with me or my "weird" violin.

After several months passed, I returned the violin to the kindly shop owner who had made it and loaned it to me. Our agreement had been that I would keep it "For as long as you play it." I didn't talk about the inexperienced school teacher who had used poor judgment in class one day. I did, however, tell him at length of people's comments about how beautiful the instrument was.

Before I left his shop, the wise old man asked me, "Are you giving up music, son?" I told him about my wonderful class with Mrs. Berman and how much I enjoyed choral music. "Maybe I was meant to be a great baritone rather than a violinist," I kidded.

"Life has handed you a very important lesson," he said. "Sometimes we may be bitterly disappointed because our well-thought-out plans come crashing down. But, as you have learned, something much better came along because you rejected defeat and kept a positive attitude while you searched for a different solution."

Did You Know?

🖋 As students go through school, they can pursue interesting courses such as music, art, dance, and drama classes. These electives can enrich one's education and life.

🖋 Sometimes a student may have a difference of opinion with a teacher. Rather than harboring any resentment, he should go to the teacher and discuss the problem. Often times, it turns out to be a simple misunderstanding.

🖋 Testing our interests in life is normal at any age. Not caring for a particular activity does not mean failure; it's just a gentle nudge to keep looking for what we are truly interested in.

🖋 Sometimes a student will have an outstanding teacher like Mrs. Berman who taught glee club and choral classes. Whatever the subject, we often remember teachers like her for the rest of our lives.

Fifteen

PAIN, PAIN, GO AWAY

The Four Musketeers (Carolyn, Virginia, Mike, and I) were sitting at our table outside the school cafeteria eating lunch. We all brought our bag lunches from home, because it saved us time not waiting in the food lines with the rest of the kids. Also, there was no need for me to spend precious money on lunch at school when I could make sandwiches and bring them from Bill's Place. Bill was a generous man, and he treated me like family.

One day I was eating a small bag of mixed nuts that the restaurant used on top of ice cream sundaes and other desserts. As I chewed on the nuts, a popping sound came from my mouth. Everyone at the table heard it, and there was instant pain from one of my rear molars. I reached carefully inside my mouth and pulled out a piece of tooth. I had broken a tooth, and the pain was intense!

"Walter, are you all right?" Carolyn asked with concern. "Did you break a tooth?"

Fighting back the pain, I nodded as I examined the piece of tooth. I put it in my pocket just as the bell rang.

"I'm okay," I said, getting up from the table. "Come on, we'll be late for class." My best friend didn't believe me, but she got up and we walked toward the brick building together.

It was difficult concentrating during my afternoon classes. The throbbing pain at the back of my jaw refused to subside. After school, I rushed home and tried putting ice on the damaged tooth, but it did little good. Mrs. Bishop came home and spotted me sitting at the kitchen table holding a towel full of ice on my jaw.

"What happened, Walter, did you get hit by something?" she asked with real concern in her voice. I explained that I had broken a tooth while eating nuts.

"I'll be right back," she said and left the room. In a few minutes she returned with a piece of paper and handed it to me. "This is the office address of Dr. Parker. His dental office is just a few blocks away on Main Street. I telephoned him and he said for you to come over and he'd see you right away. He's a good man, Walter. I've been going to him for years."

After thanking her, I left the house and headed toward Main Street. I thought my head was going to explode as I made my way through shoppers and pedestrians.

The small blue house was in the middle of the block. It was perhaps a hundred years old, but it was cheerfully painted and very well kept. "Henry Parker, DDS" the plate on the front door spelled out.

The tinkle of a small bell was heard when I opened and closed the door behind me. "You must be Walter," the lady receptionist behind the desk stated. "Come with me. Dr. Parker is expecting you."

"Hello, Walter," he greeted me. "I understand you've had an accident. Sit down in the chair, please, and let's have a look."

Dr. Parker was a kindly looking middle-aged gentleman dressed in a white smock. "Just lean back in the chair and try to relax."

After poking around my tooth with an instrument for a couple of minutes, he said, "We need to take x-rays," and I nodded my approval. *Do what you need to do*, I thought. *Just stop the pain.*

A dental technician came in and took the x-rays. She was quick and efficient. When finished, she left the room and returned in about five minutes. By now the pain from the broken tooth was almost unbearable. I didn't really care what they were going to do. *Just shoot me!* I thought.

Dr. Parker studied the x-rays on the lighted screen for a minute, and then he turned to me and said, "It's not repairable, Walter. It's got to come out." The dental technician returned with a small tray of instruments and other materials. "I'm going to give you a shot. It will sting for a second, but it will make you feel better," the dentist said.

After the injection, I felt my body begin to relax as the pain subsided for the first time in hours. After he removed the broken tooth, he stated, "Your molar broke, Walter, because there was decay under it. When was the last time you visited a dentist?"

"You're the first dentist I've ever seen, sir." Dr. Parker's eyes and his facial expression showed his disbelief.

"You're kidding," he replied. "A boy your age, a teenager, and you've never been in for dental checkups? Haven't your parents been concerned about your dental hygiene? Don't they have regular checkups?"

I told Dr. Parker that it was a long story but that my parents hadn't been around to look after my dental health. "Until recently, sir, I've lived in a number of foster homes, and this kind of thing was not high on their lists. Now I'm back living with my mom," I lied.

After the extraction, I got out of the dental chair, thanked him, and headed for the front office.

"How are we doing, Walter?" the receptionist inquired. I told her much, much better since I felt no pain with my gum still numb from the shot.

"That will be forty-five dollars, Walter," she said handing me a small piece of paper that was my bill. Before I'd left home, I had picked up five dollars from my room just in case I needed money. I had not expected dental surgery and this kind of expense over a little broken tooth.

"Ma'am, I don't have that kind of money on me. I'm a student and I work at Bill's Place, the restaurant just down the street. Is there any chance that Dr. Parker would let me pay him five dollars now and five dollars a week until his fee is paid off?"

She appeared surprised by my request. "Just a minute. I'll speak to the doctor," she replied.

In a few minutes, the receptionist returned with a confused look on her face. "Doctor told me that would be fine, Walter. He said that Mrs. Bishop has been his patient for many years, and she wouldn't send anyone to him unless they were trustworthy."

"Super!" I said. "I get paid on Saturday nights, so I'll be by every Monday with my payment. Thanks for all you and Dr. Parker have done. I really appreciate it," I added with sincerity.

The little bell on the office door rang again as I closed it and headed down Main Street. I only had a few minutes to put ice on my jaw like the doctor had recommended before I went to work.

As I walked home, I thought this would be the first time I had bought something and would be paying for it over a period of time. It felt wonderful to be part of a community and to be trusted to meet a financial obligation. Most of all, it felt so wonderful to be out of pain that I almost felt like whistling!

Did You Know?

- Boys and girls who do not have secure homes with adult care often must be responsible for their own health care issues.

- If a student has a health question, most school districts have a nurse available to come to a student's school and give advice.

- Friends, neighbors, and school staff can often be helpful because they are usually aware of what community services are available.

- Walter negotiated with the dentist when he asked him if he could pay his bill at five dollars a week rather than the entire forty-five dollars all at once. Walter was then able to financially handle an otherwise impossible situation. Learning to negotiate is an important skill.

Sixteen

KEEP YOUR PRIORITIES STRAIGHT

Walking down the hallway at school, I noticed some new posters hanging on the wall. One of them stated, "Coming Soon—End of Year Dance." It gave the date of the dance and that it was actually going to feature a live band. I needed to talk to Bill at the restaurant to make sure I could get the night off to attend the big event with Carolyn.

"Hi, Walter, got a minute?" Mr. Mason said. I stopped to find out what the assistant principal wanted. He was a good guy, and he was always there to support and help kids who might be in a jam.

"Sure, Mr. Mason. What's up?" I inquired. He told me that some of the kids on the student council had brainstormed ways to raise money for the upcoming dance. They voted on the best ideas that were presented. The winning idea was for the school to feature a lunchtime movie once a week and charge students a dime to see it. They would show it in the auditorium, and people could bring their bag lunches with them and eat while they watched a good film.

"What do you think?" he asked. I told him it sounded like a good idea and it could be a great money-maker. I asked him who was organizing and running it. "That's where you come in, my friend. Each student council member was asked to come up with the name of a student who was known to be a good organizer and one who had a solid business head on his shoulders. Guess what? Your name came up several times, and they unanimously voted for you to be the first Noon Film Director."

Hiding my surprise, I told Mr. Mason I was flattered to be chosen and asked what the job entailed. "If you accept the position, you will need to select a staff of movie ushers and ticket sellers to work for you. You will pick the film to be shown and be responsible for tracking all the money taken in. With fourteen hundred kids in this school, it could be a great deal of cash. What do you think, Walter?"

"Sounds like it could be fun. Can we do other things at the movies like sell ice cream and candy? Perhaps the PTA moms could get together and bake cookies for us to sell?"

"I can see why the council wanted you to head up this new project. Yes, to selling food and goodies. You can do anything within reason. Just let me know about it before-hand."

The bell rang as we shook hands. "Also, Walter, you're an honor roll student, so you can get excused from some of your classes when you need time to organize the film festival. There's another desk in my office that is now officially yours."

During the coming weeks, I continued to work hard on my class projects and my homework, but I really threw myself into my new job of organizing and running the weekly film festival. I asked a number of my friends to pitch in and help raise funds for the school dance. We knew hiring a live band would be a substantial cost.

Mike, Carolyn, and Virginia offered to help, and they were invaluable to the success of the project. Virginia worked with the PTA organizing cookie and brownie baking sessions after school with the mothers. Mike liked working with his group, selling and collecting tickets at the movies.

Carolyn, who was excellent at math, became our banker. She and her committee sold movie tickets in advance and also collected cash at the door. After each film day, she was responsible for meeting with the assistant principal and presenting him with an accounting of all the cash from the movie and food sales. It would be a huge job for anyone else, but Carolyn made it look easy. Her bank committee was taking in between one and two hundred dollars every week.

My days were pretty hectic. Between school and study, class projects, and also being director of the Film Festival, the days were very busy. Then, of course, my nights were taken up by my job at the restaurant. There was so little free time that Carolyn, Mike, Virginia, and I rarely had lunch together anymore. Most of my conversations with Carolyn were usually either between classes or at film meetings in the assistant principal's office.

That was okay with all of us, because we knew we were all working for a cause. The upcoming dance was going to be the biggest and the best ever put on by our school. The gym would be well decorated and have small tables around the room where couples could sit and enjoy the music and have a soft drink. There would be a low ceiling made up of layers of colored streamers and a bandstand bordered by flowers with several live trees in huge pots. It was going to be decorated just how we thought a beautiful nightclub might be. Plus, we had a great live band. We had done our job. We had raised more than enough cash for the dance, with maybe even some left over.

I was standing in front of the large sink at Bill's Place, washing the last of the dinner hour pots and pans. The restaurant was closed after a busy night. "Hey, Walt, how ya doing?" Evelyn asked as she walked into the back of the kitchen. "Getting all ready for the big dance coming up next month?"

It was like I had been struck by lightning! I dropped the large frying pan that I was holding and it fell into the soapy water with a splash. My committees and I had worked our tails off for weeks now and everything was going to be perfect for the dance. I knew that Carolyn and I were going to have a fantastic time.

There was one small problem, however. I had been so busy with school and work, plus organizing the films for school that I had forgotten to ask Carolyn to go to the dance with me.

Evelyn saw the horrified expression on my face. "Walter, are you all right?" she asked with real concern in her voice.

"Yes, I'm fine. It's just that I forgot something very important at school. I've got to go!" I said with urgency, taking the plug out of the sink so the water could drain. Then I gave the frying pan a quick rinse and dashed out the door.

Carolyn only lived a few blocks away and I needed to speak with her in person rather than on the telephone. I'm sure I broke a cross-country track record as I ran those streets to her house at full speed.

Taking her front steps three at a time, I landed in front of her door. I rang the doorbell several times before it opened. "Hello, Walter. My, you seem to be out of breath. Are you all right?" Carolyn's mom inquired. I assured her that I was just fine, and asked if I could please speak with Carolyn.

My best friend and the most beautiful girl at school came to the door. "Hi, Walter, come on in."

"Carolyn, could you come outside for a minute so we could talk? We could sit here in the rocking chairs." She came out on the porch and closed the door behind her. She had a puzzled look on her face because she knew me well, and she could see something was really bothering me.

"It's hard to know where to begin," I started. "You know how crazy life has been at school these past months working for the film festival and all. I'm so used to being with you, I mean I'm so comfortable being with you, that I feel I sometimes take things for granted." I thought I could see a faint smile beginning to form at the edges of her lips.

"What I'm trying to say is, I really screwed up. We were all so focused on raising money for the dance and planning the decorations and hiring the band that I forgot the most important thing of all. I forgot to ask you to go with me! I guess in my weird little brain I just assumed we were going together since you're my best friend and we're sort of a couple.

"I know that you are one of the most attractive girls at school, probably the prettiest, and dozens of guys would love to take you to the dance. So, are you going with someone else?" I finally got out, totally dreading the answer.

"Walter, I know how involved you can get in things. Yes, I was asked to go to the dance, and by more than one boy." My sweet friend smiled at me and added that she had given all of her suitors the same response: "Thanks for asking me, but I'll be going to the dance with Walter."

Man, what a relief! I felt a huge weight had been lifted off of my shoulders. It was getting late, and we both needed to get back to our homework. We hugged and said good night as she went inside her house. I whistled all the way home as I pondered another of life's little mysteries.

I must be one of the stupidest guys in the world. During all of my efforts to make the dance a success, I had forgotten the most important thing—my best friend. Fortunately for me, her mind had not been clouded by all that was going on. She had been planning for us. She had been thinking about me.

This dance would be very important to both of us. It was our graduation dance. We would be saying good-bye to middle school. It would certainly be a dance to remember!

Did You Know?

- Walter made many new friends when he worked on the film festival and fund-raising activities for the school dance.

- Decorating for school dances and other events is a good way for students to meet and become friends with kids from other grade levels.

- Being responsible for ordering films, coordinating and selling food, and selling tickets for the lunchtime movies were tasks that allowed Walter and his friends to learn and use new planning and organizational skills.

- Working with members of the PTA and other school organizations allows students to meet members of their community.

Seventeen

DON'T DWELL ON THE PAST

June finally arrived, and so did the end-of-the-year dance. It was everything we hoped it would be. Carolyn and Virginia looked sensational in their lovely dresses. They thought we guys looked sharp in our sports coats and slacks. Virginia's dad drove the four of us to the big affair and picked us up afterward. The live band was fantastic, and everyone danced all night and enjoyed listening to the music.

Big Bill had happily given me the night off from the restaurant saying, "Sure, take off. Go have fun. Break a leg!" When he said that, I turned and I must have had a quizzical expression on my face. "No, I didn't really mean for you to break a leg. That's just a saying they use in show business. It's telling you to have a wonderful time," he explained.

During the first lazy days of summer, I spent time on the beach. Sitting alone on my towel, I had time to reflect. Thinking about the dance and Carolyn made me smile and feel warm inside. My thoughts shifted to the clothes I had worn to the dance, my slacks and sports coat. It was wonderful that I now had enough money to buy clothes. If it weren't for my jobs these past months, I probably would have gone to the fancy affair wearing an old pair of jeans.

With clothes on my mind, I remembered some of those years when I had lived in foster homes. My shirts and jeans would become so old and torn that I was ashamed to wear them to school. There was one time during the fifth grade that I used scotch tape from teachers' desks to patch up the tears in my pants. Or sometimes I would actually use paste from the big jar at the back of the room to try to mend a rip in my shirt. I wondered what had happened to the money my foster parents received for the purpose of buying me clothes.

Shaking my head in disbelief at those memories, I forced out a little laugh. I'll bet I looked ridiculous in my near rags to some of the teachers and the other kids. "However, then was then and now is now," I said aloud. Mr. Mason had sometimes used that phrase at school during our movie meetings. I thought it was a terrific statement about letting go of the past and moving ahead with determination.

When I left the beach, I took a casual stroll through town and walked about a mile or so. Passing a place called Paul's Supermarket, I paused and looked in through the window of the large store. There were a couple of things that I needed to buy, including cereal for breakfast. Inside the store I was searching the cereal aisle for my favorite brand when I heard a voice behind me. "Hey, I know you. Aren't you the boy who works at Bill's Place?" Turning, I saw a short man with dark hair. He had a big smile on his face. "Hi, I'm Paul. This is my store. What's your name?"

I told the kind-looking store owner who I was and we stood and chatted for a few minutes. "I've known Bill for years. He runs a great restaurant, probably the best in town." Paul continued on, talking about why people like to eat at certain restaurants or shop at particular stores. "It's all about customer service," he concluded. "If you treat people right and run an honest business, they'll beat a path to your door."

He told me that he'd been in the grocery business for over twenty years. "I started as a box boy, worked my way up, learning the business step by step, and now I own and operate all of this," he said with pride.

To say the least, Paul was a very positive and enthusiastic person. *One could learn a lot from someone with his kind of charisma and self-confidence*, I thought.

"But enough about me," Paul said. "Bill sat down at our table the other night in the restaurant. You were collecting dishes and washing off tables. When I commented on you, he said you were one heck of a good worker!"

I thanked Paul for telling me this. I told him that I loved working at the restaurant and that Bill was a great boss and a good friend.

"You're on summer break, aren't you Walter? We're short one box boy here at the market. One of the fellows moved to another town. Would you be interested in giving the job a try? You could work a few hours every day and still keep your job at Bill's at night. When school starts again, if you like what we do here, you might want to think about making this your work home and give up the restaurant business for a while."

I thanked him and took a minute to think about what he'd just said. The market was a little farther away from my house than the restaurant. Then Paul told me how much my hourly pay would be. It was more than twice what I earned as a busboy at the restaurant!

"That sounds great, Paul. I'd love to work for you this summer. But I want to be honest. I'm going to tell Bill that I'm working here, holding down a second job."

"I wouldn't want it any other way," he replied. "Bill told me you were always a straight shooter."

Shaking hands with my new boss, I found my box of cereal and headed for the cash register. As I looked around, my new place of employment already had a nice feel to it. It would be neat to have the chance to learn the grocery trade.

Walking home from the store, I thought about my conversation with Paul. He was such a nice man, and he reminded me of Bill in many ways. Bill was much older than Paul, but they both had a lot in common. They both readily showed that they cared about other people. The two men were not negative or downtrodden in any way. Both were happy and energetic, and so upbeat and positive in their conversations. The way they conducted themselves made kids like me want to be like them. I guess you could say they were great examples of success—the kind of people that others want to imitate.

When I got home, I put my cereal box in my little kitchenette, walked out on the front porch, and sat down with Mrs. Bishop. I related my day at the beach and finding another job when I went grocery shopping. Over the months and now years, I had become very close to my landlady. Little by little, I had shared a number of stories about my early childhood.

"Paul sounds like a fine man," she said in her grandmotherly way. "Learning the grocery business should be a good opportunity for you, Walter, but don't take on too many hours of work when school starts. Promise?" Nodding my head, I leaned over and gave her a little hug.

A big orange sun was setting over the ocean as I told her about my flashback memories earlier in the day. How peaceful it had been on the beautiful beach, but then I had become a little sad when I remembered how bad some of my foster homes had been.

I asked her if it was possible for a person to just start over, to block out the memories of your old life. "Those were bad years," I said, "and I hate it when they pop into my mind."

Mrs. Bishop continued rocking in her chair as she listened to my concerns. "Walter, those memories of your early childhood will fade in time. But remember, we do learn from the past. Some of the people you lived with were certainly losers who had few high standards or values. But just look at all you learned from them! You are one of the most positive people I have ever known. Those old nightmares that haunt you will soon pass, so think about that great, big, beautiful world out there that's just waiting for you."

Did You Know?

🖋 Being aware of what has gone wrong in our lives can allow us to not make those same mistakes again. It also helps remind us to avoid those people or circumstances that caused the problems.

🖋 Many things that happened during our early years were positive in nature. We should try to focus on those events and build upon those early successes.

🖋 Some of the people who might have caused us problems in the past were often plagued by extreme difficulties in their own lives.

🖋 We have all faced hardships of one kind or another in our lives. The solution is to acknowledge this, think positively about the future, and move on.

Eighteen
YOU MUST SET GOALS

Because I was so busy, the summer seemed to fly by. During the day, I worked at Paul's Supermarket stacking cans of fruit and vegetables on shelves and keeping rows of toilet paper, napkins, and paper towels neatly in place. In the evening, I went to Bill's Place for another shift of clearing tables and washing dishes and pots and pans.

One day, Carolyn and her mother came by the store. Sadly, she had come to say good-bye. Her mom had found a good job with medical benefits in Bend, Oregon, where her grandparents lived. Carolyn was upset to be leaving Sea View, but happy with her mom's new job and the opportunity to live near her grandparents.

Because we had both been so busy with our jobs, Carolyn and I had drifted apart over the summer. However, as we hugged good-bye, I hated the thought of losing such a special friend.

It was almost time for school to begin again, and I was facing a critical decision. Bill and the ladies who served at the restaurant were like family to me. They had helped and supported me as I worked my way through middle school. Being able to eat at the restaurant was also a wonderful asset to a hungry, growing boy. But high school classes required more study time. I needed the evening hours when I was busy at Bill's Place.

"Bill, I need you to find a replacement for me," I said, struggling to get the words out. I had asked him if he could give me a minute to talk after closing time. As we sat together in a comfortable booth, he sipped on a cup of coffee and I had a cola. I explained that I knew I couldn't handle school and both of my jobs.

"Having time to study every night is really important to me now, Bill. The afternoon job at Paul's store fits my high school schedule better. I guess I'm just not smart enough to get by without hitting the books every night. I hope you understand," I concluded, searching his face for a sign.

"Walter, I'm surprised that you've stuck with this night job all of these years," Bill responded. "You've only missed one night when you took off to attend the school dance. Oh, yes, you did miss one of your shifts the day you almost drowned in the ocean," he added with a smile. "You've been a terrific employee, and Evelyn and the rest of the ladies are going to cry when they hear you're leaving. And," he added, "there will be plenty of customers who will be upset too when they find out you're gone."

I tried to explain how I thought of all of them as family, but it was too difficult. "You are family, Walter, and I love you like a son. Please let me know if I can ever help you in any way."

After giving my boss and good friend my two-week notice, he gave me a big hug and walked me to the door. When I was outside in the cool ocean air, I was glad that this was not my last night, that I had two more weeks to work with and say good-bye to my dear friends at the restaurant.

The next day, I told Paul that I had given the restaurant my notice. He said Bill had phoned him and told him.

"I know that was a tough decision, Walter, but Bill certainly understands, and he thinks the world of you."

As time passed, I was happy I had made this decision. I was a little insecure about leaving the restaurant because it was like a cornerstone in my life. It was a place of refuge and support from my friends and fellow employees. Leaving there, I had an empty feeling in my stomach, a sense of loneliness and sadness. But I knew in my heart that one door was closing and a new and bigger door was opening for me at the supermarket. However, my decision had been based on the fact that I needed my evenings to study and prepare for college.

School opened that year, and nearly two thousand kids were fresh and ready to bring on their high school days. My college prep courses were all interesting and challenging. By doing my homework and school projects every night, I found my classes were all going well. The only difficulty that I had experienced in high school so far was with good old algebra. However, after a couple of weeks of really focusing and a little help from my teacher, everything fell into place. Algebra turned out to be one of my favorite classes.

School was buzzing along great, and so was my job at the supermarket. My only real regret during my middle school and high school years was the fact I was unable to participate in the school's sports programs. I loved all of the major sports, and if it hadn't been for my jobs, I would have gone out for some of them.

When the final bell rang at the end of the school day, dozens of guys headed for the football field to work out, and many of the girls practiced with their volleyball or basketball teams in the gym. Paul's Market was only a short walk a few blocks away from school. However, some days they were sad walks for me, because I would rather have been back playing with the kids.

But by the time I reached the market, there was always a smile on my face, because it was a busy and fun place to work. Paul was a master at running a large market. He liked people, and he knew what they wanted to buy. I was very lucky that he was teaching me the trade.

One day I was stacking watermelons on a large table in an attractive design. When I finished, I put a sign on them that read, "Fresh Melons—50 cents each." As I stepped back to admire my artistic layout, Paul walked up and stood for a minute looking at the melon display. "Nice job, Walter," he said. "Looks great. Let me show you how we can make it even better so we'll sell more melons."

He pulled a black felt pen out of his apron pocket and wrote something under the price sign that I had just made. When he finished, the sign read, "Fresh Melons—50 cents each. Limit—only two to a customer."

"I suppose you're wondering why I added the word 'limit,'" Paul said. "I did it because most customers looking over our melons intend to buy just one of them. They had never even considered purchasing two, until they learned there was a shortage of them, as if these were all we had to sell. Usually, Walter, if you write 'limit two,' or 'limit three per customer,' most shoppers will go for the larger number. It doesn't seem to matter whether the product is watermelons, paper towels or sacks of dog food. If there's a limit on it, it seems to be human nature to want to buy it while they can."

As the weeks and months passed, I was promoted from restocking shelves to customer service, where I helped people out to their cars with their bags of groceries. It was a fun job, because I liked people and found them all interesting. It was also a good move because I didn't have to do the heavy lifting, which involved carrying cases of products out from the storage area at the rear of the store and stacking them on the shelves.

My job at the supermarket was fun, and I was learning a great deal. I had also been substituting as a cashier on occasion, and now I spent most of my afternoons after school behind a cash register.

Paul was already telling me that I could own my own business someday and become rich. "Just keep on doing as well as you're doing, Walter. Finish high school, and then you can come and work here full time. In a few years, when you're ready, you can open your own market. You're a smart guy, and you really don't need to waste your time going to college."

His last words rang through my ears like a loud alarm, and I continued to hear them as I walked home after work. "You don't really need to waste your time going to college."

I liked Paul very much. He was good to me and was teaching me all that he knew about the grocery business. My pay was good, and I was appreciative of all he was doing. However, I knew that sometime soon we would have to go our separate ways.

The talks I had with teachers and counselors through the years had really helped me to focus on a goal. That goal included finishing high school and attending college. Even though I was earning good money, I was determined more than ever to complete that goal. If owning a grocery store was meant to be in my future, it would have to wait its turn.

Did You Know?

- If students lack determination, there are many things that can tempt them from attending college.

- Paul, the grocery store owner, tried to tempt Walter to drop any plans for college by offering him a full-time job and the prospect of owning his own store in the future.

- The longer a student stays in school, the more time he will have to explore his areas of interest and decide what career is best for him.

- Some students decide to enter the work world after graduating from high school and have gone on to become very successful.

Nineteen

FEELING BAD
ABOUT WINNING

There are many neat things about going to school. One of the best aspects of being a student is the wide range of personalities one meets. Some of my teachers have been nothing but serious, following the course material closely and never giving a peek at their real personalities.

However, I had a history teacher named Mr. Buckner who should have been an entertainer. When he delivered a history lesson, you never forgot it. He stood in front of the class and quoted history like he was on the stage of a New York theater, and the class was his audience. When he talked about President Lincoln, he sounded like him and almost took on his appearance. "Four score and seven years ago," were words that we would never forget.

Sometimes some of the guys in the class would come into the classroom and sit down just as the bell rang. Once in awhile they would continue laughing over something funny that had happened, or they would continue to whisper among themselves.

"Unless you boys in the back want to spend the rest of the year making big rocks into little rocks, I suggest you put a zipper on it!" he would say to them in a stern voice.

At the beginning of the year, when Mr. Buckner first used that line, he told us it was an old saying used by prison guards telling their inmates that they had better shape up or they would be using heavy sledge hammers all day breaking large boulders into small rocks. Our history teacher used a great accent when he used that line to bring the class to order. All of us kids thought it was hilarious, and we always shut up and sat still.

Mr. Buckner was a wonderful actor, and he tried to appear mean-spirited and gruff at times. However, he was one of the most popular teachers in school. Kids were always quoting him in their little groups at lunchtime.

During the last week of school, he became uncharacteristically quiet as he stood before our history class. "You're a great group of students," he said. "I've loved every minute with you. I know I've kidded you a lot, but I want to leave you all with this very serious thought."

As he looked at us he continued, "You are all bright young people. You have everything going for you. So just remember this: Any young person who is bright, has good health, and is hardworking has the whole world by the tail." We knew he was saying that we could do anything we wanted to do and become anything we wanted to be.

During middle and high school, I was fortunate to have many terrific teachers. I also made a lot of wonderful friends. One student turned out to be one of my best friends and would remain a close buddy for years.

Richard was a couple of years older than I was. I had known him for several years when I was involved in school activities. We shared many common interests, but most important in his life was his love of flying. He was a senior when I was a sophomore, and he told me that he had been taking flying lessons for a long time.

He completed his first solo flight when he was only sixteen, and now he had logged many hours in the air flying different types of aircraft. He was such a good pilot that he was invited to join the local Civil Air Patrol. This group of private citizen aviators would participate in searches when a plane was reported missing.

A small airport was near the beach at the south end of town. Nothing big flew in or out of it, just privately owned crafts like Beach Crafts or Piper Cubs. There were also a few military training planes that could be rented by licensed pilots. Richard worked at the airport on weekends, so as an employee, he got a terrific deal on renting planes.

My favorite plane was the old World War II trainer called the PT 19. This beautiful machine was a lower, single-winged beauty with two open cockpits. There was a hole on top in the front for the pilot, and a second open cockpit a few feet behind for the student pilot. Every time Richard got a little extra money, he would run down to the airport and rent that plane. Most of the time he would ask me to go up with him.

He recognized my love of flying my first time up, and over the coming months, he gave me instructions so eventually I could fly the plane on my own. He would rent the PT 19 sometimes on weekends. We'd put on our leather helmets and goggles and take it out over the ocean and do spins, loops, and barrel rolls. The tough old plane reacted to commands so quickly that we'd almost get dizzy doing the aerobatics.

Once in awhile, we would take it up to ten thousand feet and force it straight up until it could climb no more. Then it would go into a stall, as pilots call it, and we would plunge straight down toward the ocean, with the wind screaming in our faces until we would pull it up and level out again.

What beautiful days those were! What wonderful flights! Two teenaged boys alone in the heavens, flying like birds. There were no glass roofs over our little cockpits. Our heads and shoulders were out in the open above the plane's surface, and the breezes hit us square in the face.

Sometimes we would flip the old fighter trainer over on its back so we were flying upside down. Now that was fun! We would hang upside down with nothing but our seat belts keeping us from falling out. We could look straight down at the blue Pacific Ocean sometimes less than one hundred feet below us.

As a sophomore, I continued to enjoy extra-curricular activities at school, and I decided to run for student council. With two thousand students, it was pretty difficult to get around and introduce myself and ask everyone to vote for me. Like the other candidates, I hung a couple of posters around the campus advertising my candidacy, but that didn't seem like enough.

"I've got a great idea, Walter," Richard said to me one day at school as we were talking about the upcoming election. There was just one week left before the vote, and we needed to do a better job of promoting my name. "Let's cover the campus with leaflets," he said. I thought that going around school throwing out voter flyers was a stupid idea.

"No, that's not what we're going to do. We're going to print up thousands of leaflets, take them up in the PT 19, fly over the school, and throw them out while the kids watch them float down with the breezes. We'll do it at lunchtime when they're outside eating at tables or on the lawn. It'll be a great stunt, and the air show is sure to get you elected."

Even though I had some reservations about Richard's scheme, we spent the following days on the student body copy machine producing "Vote for Walter" flyers. On the day before the election, Richard drove his dad's pickup truck to school and then to the airport before lunch. We slid open the hangar door where the old fighter trainer was housed and pushed it out on the tarmac. We loaded the bags of flyers in the back seat where I always sat.

"Contact," Richard said as he sat behind the controls in the pilot's seat. I was standing in front of the plane with my hands on its large propeller, and I repeated the command "Contact." I then spun the big prop with all my might. The engine fired immediately, and the propeller spun fiercely as I quickly backed away from it.

Climbing in the rear cockpit, I buckled my seat belt and settled in. It was rather crowded because of the thousands of leaflets jammed into paper bags. We roared down the runway, becoming airborne in seconds. Banking sharply over the ocean, we headed toward the high school which was only about two minutes away by air.

Richard circled the campus one time, and we could easily see all the kids eating their lunches outside. He signaled to me to have the sacks up and ready, and then he dropped the left wing. We swept down toward the brick buildings below. The students looking skyward, pointing as they heard the roar of the fighter trainer overhead.

I began dumping the leaflets the second we approached the outskirts of the campus, because I knew they would blow and drift down for some distance. I could see the top of the flagpole just below us as I dumped the last bag overboard. Richard pulled the nose of the plane up into a steep climb, and we sped away from our fellow students. As we made the short trip back to the beach and the airfield, I was still thinking about how close we were to the top of the flagpole when we had buzzed the campus.

Richard made his usual perfect landing. He taxied up to the hangar and shut down the engine. We had just opened the hangar's big sliding door when we heard sounds behind us. We looked back just in time to see two police cars come to a skidding halt in front of the door.

"Were you boys flying this plane above the school just now?" one of the uniformed officers asked in a loud voice as he approached us. We admitted that we had been, and he said, "You're under arrest!"

At the police station, we got out of the patrol car and entered the building. For the next hour, we tried to explain that we were only distributing flyers for the school election and that I was running for a seat on the school council. The police chief told us we had flown well below the legal altitude that planes are permitted to fly over cities. The thought of the top of the flagpole flashed through my mind. I had been busy dumping flyers, but we probably had been flying a little low.

After two hours and a phone call from the police to our high school principal, we were allowed to leave with a warning and were told all charges against us were being dropped. We had made a big mistake and were lucky that Richard and I were both good students with no trouble in our backgrounds.

Richard's dad came to pick us up, and we apologized to the police officers as we left. The following day I asked to see our principal, and we talked for a few minutes. The kids at school thought the plane buzzing the campus was a super event, followed by the waves of leaflets floating slowly to the ground.

I offered to withdraw my name as a candidate because of the flying incident. After a short lecture, the principal told me that we had used poor judgment coming in so low over the school, but all had ended well, and it was a closed issue.

Election day came, and for whatever reasons, I won. Working on the student council was certainly worthwhile and rewarding. Among other things, we had a number of fund-raisers and raised money for two college scholarships for deserving students.

However, sometimes during my term of office I was haunted by the memory of our stupid flight over the campus. I wondered if that show business type stunt had helped me win the election. Then, who knows, maybe I could have been elected on my own merits. I'll never know.

Did You Know?

🖋 Mr. Buckner was the kind of teacher that often reached students through humor.

🖋 What did Mr. Buckner mean when he said, "Any young person who is bright, has good health, and is hardworking has the whole world by the tail?"

🖋 Was the boys' plan to get student votes by flying over the school and dropping pamphlets at a low altitude a good idea?

🖋 Should the school principal have removed Walter's name from the school election?

Twenty
TO BE RICH OR RIGHT

People sometimes say that time flies when you're having fun. This was certainly the case during my years at Sea View High. Not only were they fun, but they were wonderfully productive years filled with many great teachers who imparted their wisdom and opened my imagination to the joy of living in this beautiful world.

Many of us seniors were in the process of firming up our college and career goals. Some days one of my pals would say, "I've decided to go into television. I'm going to be a sports broadcaster and do all of the big college football games, including the Rose Bowl."

The next week that same buddy would tell me that he'd changed his mind, that he had decided to become a commercial pilot for a major airline. The fact was, he really didn't know what he wanted to do. Finally, he made the correct decision by enrolling in college in a liberal arts program that would give him more time to study and gather information about various occupations and careers and what they offered.

Mike had also decided to go to college and to major in business administration. He planned to join his dad in the family business when he graduated.

Virginia had always been interested in women's fashion and design. She had selected a well-known school in Los Angeles that offered the kind of coursework that would prepare her for that kind of career.

During my junior year, I continued to work after school and on weekends at Paul's Supermarket. I became a full-time checker behind the cash register. My weekly paycheck was very good and allowed me to pay all my expenses.

However, that summer something happened at the grocery store that came as a real surprise to me. There was a large butcher shop located on one side of the market. It was owned and operated by Mario, and it was completely independent from the supermarket.

Mario was a genuine character, loud and friendly. He ran the shop, along with the help of four other butchers he employed. I learned early on that people who cut, display, and sell meat for a living don't like to be called "butchers." They prefer to be known as meat cutters. They are quick to explain that they are hired and work as apprentices for six months before they are licensed as "Journeymen Meat Cutters" by their union.

It was a Sunday afternoon during a lull in activity at the store. Mario came in and spoke to his employee behind the meat counter and then walked over to where I stood behind the cash register.

"Walter," he began, "I've been watching you for a couple of years. You've grown into a first-class worker. Why don't you quit this Mickey Mouse grocery business and come with me and learn a real trade?"

I thanked the very successful shop owner and asked for time to think it over. I had worked for Paul for years now, and perhaps it was time to learn something new. Later, when I talked it over with Paul, he said some nice words about not wanting to lose me, but then he added, "Give it a try. Maybe you'll like it."

Two weeks later, I was dressed in a long-sleeved white shirt, a snow-white apron, and was wearing a white cap on my head. "See," Mario teased, "you already look like a meat cutter!"

The first thing I learned was to carry those heavy one-hundred-forty-pound quarters of beef from the walk-in refrigerator where they hung, out to one of the big cutting blocks in the market. They called those back breakers "quarters" because they had cut the entire steer up into only four pieces. Talk about building up one's back and shoulder muscles. Carrying those beef carcasses will do it!

Next, I learned to sharpen knives. The meat market had knives of all shapes and sizes, and Mario always said, "A dull knife is a dangerous knife!" He meant that if a knife blade is dull, it might slip or jerk during cutting and injure the meat cutter.

I had worked after school and on weekends for Mario for just about a year. He had been very good to me and was a great teacher. I took and passed the union's meat cutting test on my first try, and for months I had been earning full pay as a journeyman. My weekly paychecks were huge, I thought, more than I ever imagined I would earn. Every Monday after school, I stopped at the bank and put money in a savings account for college. It was fantastic to watch it grow!

Finally, my high school days were coming to a close. I had taken the previous Saturday off from work. The University of California at Berkeley had scheduled an examination at Sea View High. It was called the English 1A exam, and it was given to all students who had been accepted by the University to determine the level of their English language skills. If you passed, you would be assigned to an advanced

English class at the University. If you failed, you had to pay the piper and take a beginner's course.

When I walked into the school library, there were only two other kids there to take the exam. A nice lady handed each of us several sheets of paper and pencils and told us to write an essay about something interesting that had happened in our lives. We were given one hour to complete the assignment.

While I sat there trying to think of something, I remembered a song that had been playing in the store when I left. It was an old tune called, "Sweet Georgia Brown." Having nothing better in mind, I used that as my essay title and made up a story about living on a farm and having a baby calf that I named Sweet Georgia Brown. I wrote how I loved her and took great care of her. She loved me equally, and when she was a year old, she won first place at the county fair and received a blue ribbon.

Several weeks later, I received a letter from Berkeley, California. It said, "Dear Walter. Congratulations on passing the University's English 1A exam, and welcome to the freshman class at the University of California." I let out a big whoop of joy at being accepted! I was thrilled!

One Saturday, Mario came by the meat market at closing time. I had just raked up the sawdust on the floor and had already cleaned the glass in the showcase.

"Come on, Walter, I'm taking you out to dinner," he said. This invitation came as a complete surprise, but I liked my boss and was happy to accept his kind offer.

As we sat down in the small diner just down the block, he said, "There's something I've been wanting to talk to you about."

A young man offered us menus and told us about the daily specials. Mario continued when the man left. "I'm not getting any younger. I've been in the meat business for twenty years. My wife and I have been talking a lot lately, and we have decided that I should hang up my apron in about ten years."

Our clam chowder arrived, and I began eating as Mario continued talking, all of the time waving both his hands. We all teased him a lot because his hands always were moving when he spoke. The guys at the store bet that he couldn't say a complete sentence with his hands secured in his pants pockets.

"You're about to graduate from high school. I know you've done well at school, but you've also been a super employee for Paul at the market, and now me at the butcher shop. Here's the deal. I think college is great for some kids. Many of them don't know what they want to be when they grow up, and college gives them more time to think. But you, Walter, you became a full-fledged meat cutter the first time you took the test. Our customers love you and want you to wait on them when you're at the market.

"I've done well financially as a shop owner. I have four employees, and the shop is open seven days a week. Money wise, I probably make about as much as some doctors. So, here's the sixty-four-thousand-dollar question, Walter. When you graduate in a few days, I want you to go into business with me and become my equal partner. You can buy your half of the shop with monthly payments from your paycheck. Then, in ten years, as half owner, you can buy out my half interest in the business and I can retire.

"This is one heck of an offer for a kid your age to get, but I like your style, and I trust you completely. Together, we could be the biggest meat-selling business in the area. And, the best part, it's here and now for the taking. You don't have to go off to college somewhere and hope you'll become successful. This is a winning proposition, and it's all yours right now!"

I had stopped eating my chowder after he had delivered his opening statement. The expression on my face must have shown Mario that I was in complete shock! The rest of our dinner came, and for a few minutes, we sat there and ate in silence. "What do you think? Does a guarantee of being rich sound good to you?" Mario finally asked.

Placing my silverware on my plate, I pushed it away from me. "Mario, I don't know what to say. You've done so much for me, and now to also offer me a partnership in the business. Man, it's such a wonderful gesture, such a great honor, and I thank you from the bottom of my heart! But even though this would be a sure thing as a career, a future and a total win-win opportunity, I've got to pass."

Mario's mouth literally dropped open, and his eyes were wide with shock at my statement.

"My life, Mario, has been a bit of a bumpy road, as you and Paul know. To survive, sometimes I had to make promises to myself. I had to set goals for myself and swear that I would keep pursuing them no matter what happened to me.

"I don't know what's going to be happening four or five years from now. However, I do know that I'm already lucky to have been accepted by a wonderful university. To have this opportunity to go to college was a major part of my goal. It's funny. It's as if I've been on a weird journey, and I can't stop now. I need to complete my goal of attending college. It's very important to me. I really hope you understand!"

Did You Know?

◻ Mario tried to tempt Walter to drop his plans for college. New events in our lives can influence us to change our goals. We must not do so without long and thoughtful consideration about what we really want to achieve in the future.

◻ What we earn as income for the work we do must be balanced with the satisfaction we get from the job. Job satisfaction has proven to be very important in our careers.

◻ Students who graduate from high school and college will enjoy many freedoms, such as where they want to live and the people they want as friends.

◻ High school and college graduates will have acquired greater knowledge and will be able to both enjoy and make greater contributions to society.

Twenty-one

GRADUATION: A DAY TO REMEMBER

It was a warm, sunny day in the beautiful little beach community when the graduating class of Sea View High, dressed in dark blue caps and gowns, paraded onto the school football field. About five hundred excited seniors were sitting in their folding chairs on the grassy field while their friends and families sat proudly in the stadium grandstands above them.

Some of their classmates would not be with them, because they had either dropped out of school or were not able to complete all their graduation requirements. They would be missed, but a number of them would earn their diplomas later at night school or during summer classes.

However, for those present, it was exciting and joyous to experience the end of a long journey. Many students had thought this day would never come as they worked their way through their high school years.

Finally, the school band began to play, and the graduation program began. The school principal and members of the teaching staff stood on a raised stage, and one by one, they called out names as students crossed the stage to receive their diplomas and handshakes of congratulations.

My name was finally heard over the public address system, and I climbed the stairs and walked across the stage. I smiled and said thank you to the principal and his staff as we shook hands and he handed me my diploma. Kids sitting in my row of seats were abuzz when I returned and sat down.

We had done it! It was over! We had graduated, and now we could go out on our own and do whatever it was that we were waiting to do. Some would take jobs at stores in town, while others would work in the oil fields on rigs or as office staff. Other students who were from farm or ranching families would go to work in their family businesses. Some of us would go off to college.

How they managed to find each other in that mob of blue gowns was a mystery, but when the last name was announced, families rushed down from the grandstands and onto the field. Within minutes, they all seemed to have found their loved ones.

I was feeling happy, but kind of sad in a way. I hated to see high school end. It was a great school with wonderful teachers, and they had made a terrific impact on my life.

"Walter," I heard my name called out in the crowd. I peered through the maze of blue gowns and saw Mrs. Bishop making her way toward me. She had a big smile on her face, and when we reached each other, she gave me a big hug. The kind and lovely gray-haired lady said, "Walter, I'm so proud of you!" I was surprised to see her. I had no idea that she had planned to attend the ceremony.

"Hey! Why are you wearing that blue cap and gown? Why don't you have your meat cutter's outfit on?" Mario joked as he joined us and gave me a big bear hug. The three of us chatted for a few minutes, and I thought all of the surprises were over, and then Paul came and joined our group.

"Hey, you looked good up there, my Walter! I took some great pictures that you can have for your scrapbook!" Paul was all smiles as he and Mario kidded me in front of Mrs. Bishop, saying what a terrible employee I had been all these years. They said the only reason they had kept me on was that nobody else wanted my job. My kindly landlady smiled politely and gave their jokes a courtesy giggle as she gently held my arm.

As the crowd began to thin out, the four of us finally said our good-byes, and I walked home with Mrs. Bishop. Later, I took her out to dinner at Bill's Place. We had a great evening, and it was wonderful to see all of my old restaurant buddies again.

The next morning, I woke up early and decided to walk down to the beach and watch the sun rise. It was a still dawn, with scarcely a breeze, which is unusual for a beach town. A flock of brown pelicans flew in a V formation just above the waves as I walked through the sand dunes. Several sand crabs ran for cover as I walked barefooted through the tide pools along the shore.

An old log that had washed up on the beach years before I had arrived was lying half buried in the sand. It was like an old friend, because I had sat on it for hours over the years while I pondered the events of the day and thought about the future. I had come to believe that there was no place in the world more peaceful or more suitable for deep thought than by the ocean.

As minutes passed, the ocean's surface took on a brighter tone as the sun crept higher in the sky. The gray foam of the breaking waves was now turning white as they crashed upon the shore. Only this rhythmic background noise, along with the occasional cry of a passing seagull, broke the silence of the dawn.

Such absolute beauty, I thought. During my time in Sea View I had become so fascinated with the ocean and its many moods that I wondered if I could ever live far from the sea. I had read about the many rhythms of these vast bodies of water and their effect upon people. This ocean and beach had been my refuge throughout my time in middle and high school, and actually from the first day I arrived there.

My thoughts flashed back to the afternoon when a kind truck driver had dropped me off just down the street. He had helped me escape from a life in a barren region where there was no friendly ocean to help me get through the hard times. I recalled the cruel old woman at the broken-down farm and the months I had barely survived there. Then, one by one, I continued to count back through my foster homes. I had stayed with a few well-meaning couples along the way, but the lion's share of my childhood was spent in houses of pain.

I shook my head in disbelief as I remembered some of the awful treatment I had endured. *So why*, I reflected, *am I not angry or bitter?*

Much of the credit had to go to my teachers in those valley schools, who helped me develop a kind of protective shield. This invisible but positive outlook on life helped me shake off many miserable days and weeks, year after year. I suppose it's like some people who seek shelter in church; I always found my refuge at school.

I reached down to pick up a few pebbles that I could skip across the tidal pools. In the water, I saw a reflection of a young man who had just graduated from high school and was now college bound.

Whatever happened to that skinny little eleven-year-old who came here in that hay truck all those years ago? I thought. He had been frightened but determined. As he had developed supportive friends at work and school, his fears had eventually turned to joy and an enthusiasm for life. With the support he had received, he had then been able to focus on school and his part-time jobs.

Secrets. He had needed to keep some secrets when he started his new life. Mrs. Bishop, his wonderful and loyal landlady, had been the first to know his secret. She had been quick to realize that Walter had no mother who would "soon" be arriving in Sea View. No, he was a youngster with no relatives to help him in his quest to grow up to be an honest and hardworking man. After hearing some of the horror stories about his foster homes, she had thrown her support to his search for a safe and secure place to live.

Evelyn, the supervisor at Bill's Place, was the next person to learn Walter's secret. Soon Bill and the other ladies became aware that Walter was "on his own," and they had joined together to make sure he was a well-fed youngster with adults who would look out for him.

Likewise, the fact that he was "raising himself" was passed from Bill to Walter's new bosses at the supermarket, Paul and Mario. All of these adults kept Walter's secret and formed an adoptive family far greater and more supportive than any Walter had ever had as a ward of the court.

That was a good one, I thought as the flat pebble I'd thrown skipped five times across the tidal pool.

Upon reflection, I was sure that several teachers at my schools had also guessed my solo status. However, none had ever questioned me about my personal life.

Tired of rock skipping, I sat down on my old log friend and gazed out at the sea, thinking of all the great friends I'd had through the years. I pictured Carolyn, Mike, Virginia, and Richard. They had all learned that I was on my own and without any family, but it hadn't affected our friendships. Even though I had lost contact with Carolyn after she and her mom had moved to Oregon, I still remembered her fondly and recalled all the adventures we'd had together. I was still good friends with Mike and Virginia, who would both be attending college in Los Angeles, and I hoped they would remain close even after I left Sea View.

Now, Richard and I were about to take off for Berkeley and the beautiful Bay Area. I felt in my heart that Richard and I would be tight buddies forever. Our flying days were over for a while, but the wonderful world of learning at the university level awaited us.

Excitement at the thought of what my future held put a smile on my face. How fortunate I had been to have all of these wonderful people on my side during my years at Sea View. I would never stop being grateful to them for reaching out to me when I needed it most.

Did You Know?

- Graduation from high school is a major milestone on the road to success.

- After high school, students will have more personal responsibility for making good decisions.

- Graduating from high school puts young people on the right track to break the poverty cycle if they come from economically disadvantaged homes.

- High school friends often turn out to be friends for life.

Twenty-Two

ALL ABOARD FOR BERKELEY

During the summer months, our beach town had its share of foggy days, but the lack of sunshine could not dampen the joy of my high school graduation. It had finally happened, and I felt fresh and excited and ready to take on the world.

Probably one of the greatest feelings of accomplishment that kids will ever experience is the personal satisfaction of a job well done when they are handed their diploma. It's one of the moments in life when we are overwhelmed by the realization that we have stuck it out and finished something really important. We have jumped through all the hoops and hurdles of middle and high school and have succeeded.

Mike's parents invited a bunch of us seniors over for a graduation dinner party. There were about twenty kids there, including my best chums. There was dancing and swimming at the party, and Mike's dad was busy at the barbecue pit. We all had a blast! It was an evening to remember and a fitting end to our high school days.

Mario had asked me to work at the meat market during the summer, which was great for me. Although I had saved money for college, I realized that I would have to continue working to finance it all the way through. Richard, my flying buddy, was also going to Berkeley, and we decided to become roommates. Richard was older and had two years of community college under his belt, so he would be entering as a junior. I, of course, would be just a freshman.

Mrs. Bishop gave me a suitcase as a graduation present. It was a super, practical gift, because I had not thought much about packing my belongings for Berkeley. I don't know, maybe I was planning on stuffing everything in cardboard boxes, but my wonderful landlady had thought ahead.

As summer came to a close, I said so long to Mario and my friends at the market. In a couple of months, I would turn eighteen, and it was time to head north to the Bay Area. Early one morning I drove to Richard's house in the old Ford I had owned for over a year. We piled his belongings next to mine in the trunk, and he hugged his tearful mom and dad good-bye. The Ford sounded great as we drove down the street, turned onto Highway 101, and headed north.

As we drove up the beach route toward Santa Barbara, I thought about Mrs. Bishop and our good-bye that morning. I could tell she was fighting back tears when she hugged me. "Walter, always remember this is your home and that I'm here for you."

My eyes were damp when I thanked her for all she had done for me over the years. "If I ever had a mother," I said, "I wish it could be you." With those heartfelt words, I had turned and walked to my car. She waved with both hands as I drove off down Oak Street, the same street I had strolled up with my worn backpack so many years before.

Richard and I took turns driving as we made our way up the highway to San Francisco. Crossing the long Bay Bridge to the East Bay was a thrill. We stopped at the toll booth where we paid the uniformed cashier. Finally, after passing the City of Oakland exit, we saw a freeway sign up ahead that read "University Avenue." Berkeley! We both let out a yell of excitement, knowing that our long drive was coming to an end.

Tired from the long trip, we pulled into an inexpensive motel where we spent the night. Up early and fresh the next morning, we drove through neighborhoods near the huge University of California campus looking for signs on houses that read "Rooms for Rent."

After several hours of talking with landlords and checking out rooms, we found an old two-story home only a block from the campus. It had a large room upstairs, with beds and desks for each of us, and it had plenty of closet space. The bathroom and shower were just outside our door. We paid our new landlady the first and last months' rent and then jubilantly unpacked the car.

The rest of the day was spent exploring the massive campus where over 20,000 students studied for their degrees. Its rolling grounds were green with grass, and many beautiful trees adorned the pathways. Richard and I were excited as we looked up at the great clock tower standing hundreds of feet above us. The Campanile. This well-known campus clock tower could be seen for miles from roads and freeways that crisscrossed the Bay Area.

For the next few days, we continued exploring Berkeley. Richard and I were looking for part-time work. We found it at a fraternity house just a couple of blocks from where we lived. About forty college guys lived at the house. We were hired to wash pots and pans for a couple of hours after the dinner meal. There was no pay involved, but they gave us a free breakfast and dinner every day, which was great!

Moving to Berkeley a week before school began turned out to be a very smart move. We were able to find good housing near the campus and jobs that provided us with most of our meals. Those are the two basic essentials that kids moving away from home for the first time should consider.

On Friday, Richard and I registered for our classes. My courses were designed for a premed major. Richard planned to become an engineer and go into the airline business someday. It was an exciting day on campus, but not nearly as thrilling as Monday morning when we were awakened by the big bells of the campus clock tower. My first day at college! My first classes at the University of California!

The first week at Cal was terrific. My professors were super, and class time whizzed by as I sat and took notes. A couple of my classes, like Psychology 1A, were so large that they had more students in them than in my entire graduating class back at Sea View High School.

Kids going off to college for the first time should consider whether they would be more comfortable in a large or a small college setting, or even at a community college close to home. Even though it can be overwhelming at first, some kids do well at the big universities, while other eighteen-year-olds feel more comfortable on a campus that looks and feels something like their old high school.

In the late afternoons, I usually headed for the gym. An Olympic-size swimming pool was located there, and swimming had become my main mode of relaxation. During the coming months, I took and passed the Red Cross Lifeguard course. Later, I was hired as a lifeguard at that campus pool.

I guess my near-drowning experience back on the beach at Sea View must have made a tremendous impression on me, because I continued to strive to conquer anything aquatic. In the spring, I enrolled in the California Water Safety Instructor program at the pool and completed it successfully. Now I had the license to manage and operate swimming classes anywhere, and also to train and qualify lifeguards.

Earning these credentials had been a long-time goal for me. Thrilled to have my name printed on swimming diplomas, I wrote a letter to the recreation department back in Sea

View. Did they need a hometown boy to work as a lifeguard for the summer on the beautiful beach at the foot of Oak Street? In my letter, I gave as references the names of my Berkeley swimming coach and the principal at my old high school in Sea View.

Richard and I found the winters in Northern California colder than those at home in the south. There was more rain and what seemed to be a chill in the air, but we eventually got used to it. During football season, we proudly wore our jackets that said "CAL" across the front as we walked up Strawberry Canyon to the stadium with thousands of other students.

Our final exams were coming in only a week, and then it would be summer break. There was a letter in my mailbox when I got home from school one day. It was from the Sea View Recreation Department. It read, "We are pleased to offer you a full-time position as lifeguard this summer on our local beach. Congratulations!" I ran upstairs yelling with joy! Soon I would be back in my wonderful little town. Soon I would be spending all my summer days on my special beach with my best friend, the ocean.

After final exams, Richard and I headed home in the old Ford. Later, I received my grades in the mail. Half As and half Bs, which I figured wasn't too bad for a young freshman at a huge university. Richard did okay, too. His mom and dad were pleased with his first year university efforts.

Mrs. Bishop had rented my old room, as we agreed she should do. I couldn't afford to pay for it throughout the school year, and she needed the income. Luckily, she did have a small room in the front of the house that was vacant. This would be my last stay at her place. In future summers, a teacher friend would ask me to house-sit his home during his absence. This would really save me money since I would not have to pay rent all summer.

Best of all, every morning I would pack a sack lunch and head off to work. Out the front door, then two minutes down Oak Street to the ocean and its white beach. Once there, I would climb the ladder to the top of the lifeguard station and wait for the summer bathers to hit the beach. I could have had my old job back at the meat market, but I wanted to work at something new and worthwhile.

Fortunately, I never had anyone drown during the summers I worked as a beach lifeguard or manager of large swimming pool programs. However, there was a close call with two teenagers my first summer on the beach. Both kids got caught in a riptide out beyond the surf line. Lucky for me, they were swimming together.

When I saw them waving their arms and screaming for help, I jumped down from the stand and ran into the surf with my torpedo shaped buoy hanging by a cord from my shoulder. As I swam out into deep water, the buoy followed me, attached to me by its cord.

Both swimmers were still afloat when I got to them. The younger girl, however, was about to go under, so I quickly clipped the torpedo buoy around her waist. Then I told her older brother to take my hand and kick, which he did. Pushing the girl riding the buoy ahead of me, we made our way toward the beach where a large wave gave us a helping push into shallow water. We were all thankful and happy to feel the sand beneath our feet.

To my dismay, I found out that first summer that many parents regularly dropped off their children at the beach. They would return for their kids five or six hours later. In their absence, they expected the lifeguard on duty to babysit and keep them safe. During one workday, I had to rescue the same six-year-old boy three times.

As the weeks of summer passed, my skin tanned to a dark brown. After the lifeguard station closed in the late afternoon, I would take long swims along my favorite beach. Far out beyond the waves, I would float quietly and listen to the seagulls crying out overhead. In the distance, I could hear the booming of breakers as they pounded the shoreline. Frolicking like a seal, there was never a place I felt safer than out there in my private ocean home.

Did You Know?

- During one's early high school years, students should begin investigating what goes into applying for and securing a college scholarship.

- Some kids need to work part time while attending college. Should they need to do so, they might want to check out the types of student loans that are available to responsible young people.

- Many students work during the summer months and save their money for future school expenses.

- Students going away to college should investigate where they are going to live. Room rentals, dormitory housing, and living with a family are some of the options. Information on housing is available at college student housing offices.

Twenty-Three

DECIDING ON A CAREER

My wonderful summer at home on the beach passed swiftly, leaving me with many memories that I will cherish for years. My friends were all back in Sea View from college, and they seemed happy and were also doing well.

In September, Richard and I took off again for Berkeley in my old Ford to begin another year at Cal. I continued with my premed major and found all my science classes still interesting and challenging. I was also taking classes in French and Italian because of my love for opera. Knowing the basics of those languages was important to understand the libretti, the words to that glorious music.

However, as determined as I was to become a doctor, something continued to nag at my subconscious. I thought that by becoming a physician I would be joining a noble cause. As a doctor, I could help poor people who needed help, people who couldn't afford medical care, like Carolyn's mother. There were masses of folks in every country who couldn't even afford to put food on their tables. For them, money for medical aid was out of the question.

But I was starting to feel that there was a sadness attached to the medical profession. Even though the personal reward of helping the needy was great, dealing with life and death every day had to take a toll on a medical professional. These were some of the deep thoughts that stuck with me as I began a new year. I knew I must resolve this issue before I got much further in my college education. If I didn't think medicine was for me and I didn't really want to become a doctor, then I needed to decide soon.

Richard and I had a tough first week of classes. We were beat, flattened, and needed some cheering up. We decided to go to San Francisco and have some fun. We didn't go to the city often because we couldn't afford it. Tonight, however, we needed to get away from this campus town and our studies.

Driving across the magnificent Bay Bridge that was all aglow with lights, we headed toward North Beach. When we arrived, we parked the Ford and walked the streets. They were packed with fun-loving people and loud music that spilled out of the clubs along the way. As we approached an old brick building, we heard loud banjo music.

Peering in the windows, we saw a joyous crowd listening to a large banjo band on the stage. The performers were dressed in bright, red-striped searsucker jackets. They were a colorful looking bunch, and they were really pounding out the music. That was my first, but certainly not my last, visit to the famous old Red Garter Restaurant on North Beach in San Francisco.

After a couple of hours of wild banjo numbers and singing by the audience, we left the club and walked the streets, taking in the nightlife and the San Francisco crowd. Finally, having had enough, we climbed in the Ford and headed back toward Berkeley. The weather was turning nasty, and the wind was blowing hard. Before we reached the Bay, it began pouring rain, and it felt like we were in the middle of a hurricane.

I could scarcely see the road as I inched the car out onto the bridge. There was almost no traffic as we crept along while the wind and the rain pounded my little car.

Suddenly, we could make out flashing red lights up ahead. The police had set up a roadblock and stopped all traffic from crossing the eight-mile-long bridge. The gale force wind was blowing so hard that Richard and I could feel the Ford swing to and fro like it was sitting on a giant swing set in a park. It was a little scary as we sat there in the pitch-black darkness with the headlights turned off. Would it be possible? Could a huge bridge like this break and crash into the San Francisco Bay with us sitting in the middle of it? We didn't think so, but we weren't taking any bets.

After an hour or so, the wind subsided and the police lifted the roadblock and let us pass. We made our way back to Berkeley and arrived there grateful to be all in one piece.

Thanksgiving break came, and Richard went home to Sea View to have turkey with his family. As I walked from my rooming house into the commercial area, I noticed Berkeley was like a ghost town with hardly anyone on the streets. Apparently twenty-thousand-plus students and professors had all gone somewhere for the holiday. I felt like I was the only one who hadn't gone home.

As I walked past Larry Blake's Restaurant, there were a few early diners inside that made me feel I was not totally abandoned. I arrived at the window of my favorite little hotdog stand and ordered a foot-long special from the young man sitting there reading a magazine. Usually, this popular eating spot was jammed with students.

"Are we the only two people left in town?" I asked him. He gestured at the empty sidewalks and quiet streets and replied that everyone else must have gone home.

I put mustard and chopped onion on my Thanksgiving dinner and walked over and sat down on the curb. As I ate, I got accustomed to the sound of silence in the usually busy college town. For a couple of minutes, I felt a little rush of sadness, probably caused by the feeling of being alone. But that depression soon passed as I battled the twelve-inch frankfurter and its bun.

Since early high school, I had pretty much gotten over any feeling of loneliness, even while living on my own. There were so many wonderful people in my life, such as Mrs. Bishop and all of the folks at the restaurant and other places where I had worked over the years. Then, of course, there were all my great friends who were there for me as we wound our way through middle and high school. They, and my teachers, were all family to me. With people like that around you, it's tough to feel alone.

In recent years, working as a water safety instructor teaching kids how to swim and survive in water, I became very fond of working with youngsters. My days with them were alive and vibrant, funny and rewarding. There never seemed to be a dull moment.

In my swim classes, I could look over the students and often spot the shy or frightened one, or the bold and brassy fellow. I would often see those faces that were intentionally masked and muted that did not want to risk showing anything. Often it had been challenging to unravel their defensive disguises and allow them to gain self-confidence and trust themselves in my care in twelve feet of water. Trusting a teacher can sometimes require a great leap of faith. However, once accomplished, the relationship can prove to be a lifesaver.

As I ate my hotdog, I remembered my thoughts during the recent months. There had been long periods of reflection about whether I should become a doctor. The more I considered medicine, the more I felt it was certainly a noble profession, but perhaps better suited for someone else.

After all, people are allowed to change their minds. Just look at my roommate and friend, Richard. He was determined to fly commercial airliners around the world for a living. Now, after close to four years in college, he'd fallen in love with—guess what? Math and taxes! Yes, he loved working with people's taxes, so he was going to be a certified public accountant—a CPA! That was great! I knew he'd be a good one. Whatever Richard did, he did well.

Now, as for *moi*, as we say in my French class. What about me? I took another bite of my Thanksgiving hotdog and pretended that I heard a drum roll inside my head. It was the kind we hear when someone's about to make an announcement.

"Boom-du-boom, boom-du-boom," the drums pounded out and then suddenly stopped.

"Walter, what is your final decision?" the announcer shouted.

In my brain, I stood before thousands of people, and I stated, "Ladies and Gentlemen, my decision is simply this. I absolutely love working with kids, so I'm going to become a teacher."

Inside my brain the crowd roared its approval, and I chuckled as I returned to reality and finished my hotdog.

When the new term at Berkeley began, I changed my major to education. I was extremely happy with this decision. With any luck, it wouldn't be long until I graduated and would be in a school somewhere doing what I loved: teaching kids!

Did You Know?

- Colleges and universities welcome kids who have overcome hardships such as poverty or growing up in foster homes.

- Some colleges have formed clubs and campus organizations for students who have come from foster homes.

- Students with special talents in areas such as sports, theater, art, and music should check out what their college might have available in the way of scholarships or support. This could include help with buying books or living expenses.

- Walter learned to trust and use schools as a safe haven while growing up. His teachers often served as substitute moms and dads when giving him advice. You don't have to be a foster home kid to take advantage of these wonderful supports. Just go for it!

Epilogue

WHAT HAPPENED TO WALTER?

- He graduated from college and became a teacher.

- He taught in the Sea View School District, alongside some of his own favorite teachers.

- Walter received a Master of Science Degree in Education from the University of Southern California.

- He was awarded a Presidential Fulbright Scholarship and traveled to Africa where he taught at an African teachers' college.

- Walter returned to the United States and became a school principal in Sea View.

- Walter married and had two daughters. He took his family back to Africa. This time he went to Nigeria where he worked as a consultant to the Peace Corps and the Nigerian Government.

He returned to California and became a department head at the University of California at Los Angeles.

The U.S. Peace Corps hired Walter as superintendent of its training centers located on several Caribbean islands. He lived in St. Thomas in the U.S. Virgin Islands.

He later returned to California where he worked at Sea View as a school district administrator.

More recently, Walter and his wife, Genny, have served as correspondents for several newspapers and written the wild adventure book, *Growing Up In Africa*.

About the Authors

L es and Genny Nuckolls are both California natives with a love for traveling and writing.

After a challenging childhood spent in many foster homes and then "on his own," Les went to college, eventually receiving a master of science degree in education. He was one of fourteen Presidential Fulbright Scholars.

Les elected to go to an African bush college near the Congo border to help train teachers. Following a stint in Nigeria as a consultant to the Peace Corps and the Nigerian government, he served in the U.S. Peace Corps as superintendent of its training centers located on several Caribbean islands.

After careers in education and administration, Les and Genny developed their passion for writing by working for several newspapers in Northern California. They have also written the book *Growing Up in Africa* to chronicle the stories Les has always loved to tell about his adventures in Africa.

For the past ten years, Les has been teaching and counseling students, many of whom are living in challenging home situations. He has found that telling his own story has encouraged and strengthened their determination to stay in school and forge a better life for themselves. This book was written for them.